CROSSBREED

Published by Dark Titan Entertainment.

Also available in hardcover and eBook.

Dark Titan Universe is a branch of Dark Titan Entertainment.

First Printing 2021.

Hardcover ISBN: 978-1-7353154-2-3
Paperback ISBN: 978-1-7363782-0-5
eBook ISBN: 978-1-7353154-3-0

darktitanentertainment.com

WORKS BY TY'RON W. C. ROBINSON II

<u>BOOKS/SHORT STORIES</u>

DARK TITAN UNIVERSE SAGA

MAIN SERIES
Dark Titan Knights
The Resistance Protocol
Tales of the Scattered
Tales of the Numinous
Day of Octagon
Crossbreed
Heaven's Called

<u>Forthcoming</u>
The Resistance/Protectors War
Underworld
Magicks and Mysticism
The Resistance vs. The
Enforcement Order

SPIN-OFFS
In A Glass of Dawn: The Casebook of
Travis Vail
Maveth: Bloodsport

<u>Forthcoming</u>
The Curse of The Mutant-Thing
Trail of Vengeance
War of The Thunder Gods

ONE-SHOTS
Maveth, The Death-Bringer
Mystery of The Mutant-Thing
Shade & Switchblade
Retribution of Cain
The Mythologists

COLLECTIONS
Dark Titan Omnibus: Volume 1
Dark Titan Omnibus: Volume 2
Dark Titan One-Shot Collection

THE HAUNTED CITY SAGA
The Legendary Warslinger: The Haunted City I
Battle of Astolat: A Haunted City Prequel (KOBO Exclusive)
Redemption of the Lost: The Haunted City II
Consequences of the Suffering: The Haunted City III (Forthcoming)

SYMBOLUM VENATORES
Symbolum Venatores: The Gabriel Kane Collection
Hod: A Symbolum Venatores Book
Symbolum Venatores: War of The Two Kingdoms
Symbolum Venatores: Elrad's Chronicles (Forthcoming)
Symbolum Venatores: Mystery of the Magician (Forthcoming)
Symbolum Venatores: Twilight of the Gods (Forthcoming)

OTHER BOOKS

Lost in Shadows: A Novel
Lost in Shadows: Remastered
Accounts of The Dead Days
The Book of The Elect
The Extended Age Omnibus
Frightened!: The Beginning
EverWar Universe: Knights & Lords

THE DARK TITAN AUDIO EXPERIENCE PODCAST

Season 1: Introductions
Season 2: In a Glass of Dawn
Season 2.5: Accounts of The Dead Days
Season 3: Battle For Astolat
Season 4: Hallow Sword: Cursed

CROSSBREED

TY'RON W. C. ROBINSON II

CONTENTS

THE ASTONISHING VOLTAGE: WAVEFRONT

I

<u>LIGHTNING ABOVE, TREMORS BELOW</u>

The city of Los Angeles has been restored to its former state. Some neighborhoods are still removing banners of Marc's New Sparta. The Voltage continued assisting the civilians of the city. Taking down muggers and thieves who look upon the public as weak targets. Much of the city thanked the Voltage for what he did concerning King Marc.

After much timing, Los Angeles has been the sight for continuous and unknown tremors circling the city. After the tremors decrease, streaks of lightning cover the skies. Meteorologists and scientist have looked into the strange phenomenon. Some accuse Voltage's actions of using his electrical power to bringing about the lightning storms. The Voltage, however, appeared unaffected by the lighting storms. The tremors increased and continued daily till the public looked at them as just another hot day.

Days later, seismologists in the city discover something peculiar moving underneath the city. Pointing its origins to the ocean. Its strength was strong and its speed moved at the mach of Voltage's own. The object appeared and moved upward toward the city. Within seconds of its discovery, a hole had burst open in the streets of Los Angeles. Out of hole spewed out water from the ocean, followed by a stronger tremor. From the hole, the object came up to the street. Walking. The object was a humanoid figure, but a hybrid creature of sorts. It let out a laugh before vanishing into electrical particles.

The creature was moving through the air and electrical currents surrounding it like a bolt of lightning. Turning its head, something caught its attention as it followed the unseen, yet, sparking trail.

II

<u>GROWING ENEMIES</u>

Dealing with the ramifications of joining the Protectors and aiding the Resistance against Octagon, Steve Walker sat in his Grandma's home as he is greeted by his friends Emily Hemsberg and Gregg Stykes. On the TV in the home was the news. Broadcasting the events of the previous night involving the tremor and the damage done to the street.

"Wonder who's gonna pay for that?" Gregg said.

"The city will take care of it." Steve replied.

"You mean us." Emily said. "The taxpayers."

"She's not wrong there." Betty said. "Now, what do you all have planned for today?"

"Nothing much." Steve said.

A knock came from the door and Steve stood up to answer. Opening the door, he sees her once again.

"You're still here?" Steve said, seeing Ava at the door.

"I am. Figured we could talk."

Ava entered the home to Emily and Gregg's surprise. Betty walked over to Ava, hugging her.

"I haven't seen you in years."

"Same here."

"How's everything? Everyone?"

"They're all doing fine. San Francisco fits them perfectly."

Emily and Gregg stood up, greeting Ava.

"Nice to see you again, Ava." Emily said.

"And I you. You too, Gregg."

"Now, Steve, I need to speak with you."

"Sure."

Steve and Ava walked into another room while Betty, Emily, and Gregg stayed in the living room. Entering the other room, Steve closed the door.

"What did you want to talk about?"

"You've been distant. Quiet on me ever since I came back."

"Because it was unexpected."

"Unexpected?"

"Yeah. I'm still trying to figure out you're still here."

"I didn't come to start a problem."

"What problem?"

"I can tell there's something going on between you and Emily."

"I don't know what you mean."

"Yeah, you do."

"Ok. I do. But, it's something we haven't figured out yet."

"You told me the same."

"That was before you left."

"But, we were close. Closer than you and Emily."

Steve sighed. Walking toward Ava. Placing his hands on her shoulders. He looked into her eyes with a grin.

"I can't balance my time with Emily and with you."

"I'm not saying you should balance it. I'm saying you have a choice to make."

"Don't do this."

"We can all be friends. I respect that. But, when it comes to who you're going to love. It's in your hands"

Ava exited the house while everyone turned to Steve. Who walked out of the room shaking his head.

"What's wrong?" Betty asked.

"Nothing."

Steve hung out with Emily and Gregg throughout the day. Going places and socializing. Upon the brink of dusk, he strange entity rose again in the city, now in the same place as Steve. Seeing the glowing figure ahead. Gregg wanted to get closer, but Emily pulled him back by his shirt. Steve stared. He already knew.

"Guys go."

"What about you?" Emily asked.

"I'm going to help these people get out of the way."

"Are you crazy?"

"Maybe."

Steve ran from the scene, changing from his civilian clothing to the Voltage. Bolting into the air and crashing down in front of the electrical entity. The two stare each other down as the remaining civilians run from the street.

"What are you?"

"I am lightning. I am water."

"I don't understand."

"Many do not."

"Why are you here? Why attack innocent civilians?"

"To bring you out. You are the energy I felt as I made my arrival."

"And what do you want?"

"Your electricity. I require its source. It is unlike anything I have encountered."

"You want my power?"

"Precisely."

"I think not, whomever you are."

"I am Sonicwave. Your death is my introduction."

"Only if you can catch me."

Sonicwave chased Voltage through the city of Los Angeles. The two only seemed like moving lightning bolts to those on the ground as the streaked from the air to the ground. However,

Sonicwave caught Voltage by his leg, causing him to crash to the street. Voltage turned over to see Sonicwave standing over him, striking him with his electric claws, scratching through his suit. Voltage stood up and delivered lightning punches to Sonicwave. He stood firm with a sinister grin.

"What are you?" Voltage wondered.

Sonicwave punched Voltage across the pavement as crowds of civilians began to pour in. surrounding the fight scene. Voltage stood up and fired electrical blasts toward Sonicwave, who absorbed them without haste. Sonicwave laughed as he fired them back, hitting Voltage in quick succession. Voltage fell to his knees as Sonicwave grabbed him, launching him into the air with a mixture of electric and water. The combination of the blast knocked Voltage unconscious as he fell and collapsed into the street.

"As I said, your death is my introduction."

Sonicwave gazed around, seeing the people and vanished with a quickening bolt. Civilians all ran over to the beaten and downed Voltage.

III

LIVING YOUR DESTINY

Steve had awoken, finding himself in a room. His room. His body ached from the battle. Bruises covered his body and the pain moved through him as he tried to move around the bed.

"How? How did I get here?"

Steve took another look and saw Ava sitting on the side of the bed. Immediately, he reached for his mask, now realizing his Voltage suit is laying near the closet door. He glanced at the suit and back to Ava.

"You know?"

"I know now."

"I'm sorry I didn't tell you sooner. Or anyone."

"You had good reasons why. Otherwise, we could've been targeted and possibly killed. All in the meaning of getting to you."

"Where's everyone else?"

"They're doing what they can to get away from that thing's havoc."

Steve sighed.

"I'm sure the police can handle him."

"I'm not so sure of that. Look what that thing did to you."

"It's not natural."

"I'm not understanding."

"It called itself Sonicwave. Said my death would be its introduction."

"And it's attacking the city because it believes you're dead?"

"Yeah." Steve said quietly. "Partially."

"What do you mean?"

"The Voltage is no more."

Sonicwave roamed through downtown Los Angeles, ransacking the city, causing havoc. The police do their best to stop the electrical creature, but noting they have is optional. Sonicwave ran through them with hydro-blasts from his hands, layered in electricity. Sonicwave let out a roaring screech which echoed through the entire city.

"The Voltage can't be dead." Ava said.

"That monster proved I am not ready for the greater battles ahead. I can't continue to try."

"But, look at the other things you've done. You helped take out the Neo-Spartan, you allied with others. You even aided in protecting us all from a walking A.I. with a messiah complex. You are a hero."

"How can you be sure of that?"

Ava nodded. She walked over and grabbed the Voltage suit and held it in front of him. Steve stared at the suit before looking back to Ava.

"Because you are The Voltage and it is astonishing."

Steve continued his stare as Ava glanced at his arms and shoulders. Seeing the bruises had vanished. No signs of them anywhere on Steve's body.

"The bruises are gone."

"I heal faster than most."

"How is that possible?"

"It's a long story."

IV

GREATER THE VILLAIN, GREATER THE HERO

Sonicwave continued his mayhem in the city. More police arrived at the scene of the havoc and Sheriff Jack Martin was with them.

"What is that?" Jack asked.

"We aren't sure." An officer replied.

"We can't take down that thing. We need The Voltage."

"Sir, he tried. Didn't work."

"There's no way."

"I'm sorry, sir."

Jack shook his head as Sonicwave spotted him and the officers. They held up their firearms speedily.

"More fodder?!" Sonicwave said.

Sonicwave rushed toward the officers and without notice, a bolt of lightning flashed through the area, striking Sonicwave, knocking him to the ground. The officers paused, seeing the creature down. Sonicwave rose up, holding his chest and grunting in pain.

"What was that?" An officer asked.

Behind them appeared the Voltage, moving toward them as the lightning himself. He stopped, revealing himself to their sight. Sonicwave stood up with a grin. Chuckling.

"Officers, leave him to me."

"But, what about what happened to you?"

"It's fine. I'll manage."

The officers flee the scene as the Voltage and Sonicwave walk in circles, facing one another.

"You had me down last time."

"It was only for a moment."

"A moment? What do you mean?"

"This is all a test. I needed to know if you're as strong as they claim."

"Who's they?"

"You'll find out very soon.

"I don't think so."

Voltage blasted a lightning bolt toward Sonicwave, who quickly vanished into a hydro-lightning bolt himself, taking off into the sky. Voltage watched as he left.

"Come on! I was ready for a rematch!"

Sometime later, Steve met with Ava and told her of his story. From the origin of his abilities to the last encounter with Sonicwave. Ava questioned while the creature would just leave the fight and spare Voltage a second time. Steve questioned it himself, replaying the words spoken by Sonicwave in his mind. He wanted to know of the others and who could they be.

BIONIC RAGE: COVERT OPERATIONS

I

LIVING WITH PEACE AS POSSIBLE

Dameon Mason rested in his home. Sitting peacefully besides the technological noises coming from his bionic limbs. He sighed. A knock came from the door. Unsure, he stood up and answered it. Seeing a man in a well-dressed suit standing before him. A clean-shaven middle-aged man with a smile. A large smile.

"You are him." The man said.

"Who would be him?" Mason questioned.

"Pardon my unannounced visitation. My name is Aaron Conroy. I have come here to specifically meet you."

"Meet me for what?"

"Well, I heard about how you handled those guys a few months back. Hell, you even teamed up with those other heroes roaming around. Twice. Now, I'm not here to cause a disturbance like the one in Retropolis or Newark. But, I have something that may interest you."

"I'm listening."

"I am offering to take the bionic technology of ours off your hands. Literally."

"You want my limbs?"

"And the glowing thing in your chest. I figure it powers the tech.”

“Yes, it does. Why do you want my bionic tech?”

“Because there aren’t many people like you, Mr. Mason. Think about it. The tech you have right now could benefit hundreds, thousands, no, millions of people across the world. An opportunity to give back to communities across the oceans.”

“I didn’t ask for these in the first place. Why would I choose to give them to those who do not know how this occurred?”

“Take it slow. I’m not trying to force you to give them up.”

“Wouldn’t work anyway.”

“That so?”

“It is. Spencer Vargas trued the same thing. Looked where he’s at right now.”

Conroy nodded. “Understood.”

“I think you already know my answer.”

“I believe I do.”

Conroy nodded, turning away from the door. He waved his finger in the air, looking back at Mason.

“This isn’t the only time we’ll encounter one another. You will see me again soon.”

“And when we do, I will tell you what you’ve just heard. Or worse.”

Conroy scoffed. Walking away. Mason shut the door. Conroy entered his car, pulling out his cell phone and dialing a number. He waited with a sigh.

“I just saw him.” Conroy said on the phone. “We need that tech. the penalty has been placed on this Dameon Mason guy.”

Conroy took a slight pause as he listened to the other end.

“You’re already in the city?” Conroy chuckled. “This is better. Much better. Then, you know what you have to do.”

Conroy put down the phone, nodded with a grin, and drove from Mason’s residence.

II

FIRST SET

Immediately after the call, Chris Stanton stood on a rooftop, overlooking the district of Greektown. Having the appearance of a soldier, yet one of austerity. His uniform was unlike most soldiers. Wearing all black. Equipped with a tactical jacket, cargo pants, and boots. He reached into his pocket, pulling out a photo of Mason. One taken from a distance. Stanton scoffed, placing the pocket back into his pocket and he took a breath, taking in the sight of the district.

Brad and Claire sat inside Mason's home during the afternoon. They spoke of the past events regarding Spencer Vargas and the incident up in Retropolis to which Mason attended.

"You have to tell us why you went up there without giving a notice."

"What was I supposed to say?" Mason asked. "That I was heading north to deal with some super powered threat?"

"You were in the midst of a battlefield." Claire noted. "In the hands of these heroes and whatever those things were coming from the sky."

"It's nothing too different that being in service."

"We never dealt with beings from other places on the field."

"But we dealt with foreign invaders. Terrorists who wanted our families and friends killed. All in the name of their gods or their laws. The same thing occurred in Retropolis with those sky-beings. They serve a power higher than themselves. They follow a different set of laws. We were their targets. Imagine what could've happened if the heroes lost."

"But, you guys didn't lose. You won."

"And what has happened since? People across the world are witnessing more of these heroes rising up. They're calling me one of them. One of the Risen."

"After what you did with Vargas and what happened in Retropolis, you are a hero."

Mason shook his head as he looked down.

"I'm not a hero. I'm a soldier."

While sitting, they hear knocks at the door to which, Clare stood up and answered the door. Seeing Nathan Armstrong outside. She saw him as she opened the door. Once the door open, Nathan smiled brightly.

"Nice to see you again, Ms. Lyons."

Nathan looked inside, seeing both Mason and Brad staring at him. He waved.

"May I come in?" He asked gently.

Claire turned toward Dameon and he gave a nod. Nathan had entry into the home. Upon entering he shook the hands of Mason and Brad. Claire sat down next to Dameon while Nathan sat beside Brad.

"What's happening now?" Mason asked.

"Same old situations. Nothing big."

"So, why come here?"

"The city is looking for you, Dameon. They need your help."

"My help? On what?"

"The things you've done in the past few months is astounding. You stopped a criminal organization from taking over this city. Plus, you managed to save the world when you went up north. The world knows of your presence and Detroit seeks your support."

Mason sighed before standing up and walking into the kitchen. Claire watched him before turning back to Nathan.

"What else can be done?"

"I don't know anything else besides what I've said. If Dameon goes outside, the people will automatically clamor him about protecting this city. Others will be in fear of him because of the bionic limbs."

"They have every right to fear me." Dameon said from the kitchen. "That's not a problem."

Elsewhere, Aaron sat inside an office. He thought on matters concerning Mason and his bionic tech. shaking his head, he took out his phone and went through the numbers. Searching for one and upon his search he stopped and called the number.

"This the man I need to speak to?" Aaron said. "Ah, good. I have a job for you. If you are interested. Here's the deal. I already have one man on the job. But, two is better. Will you take the job or let the other guy?"

Aaron sat quiet and listened. He nodded with a grin. A grin of confirmation.

"Good. Come back to me when the job's done."

Aaron placed the phone down and stood up from his desk, gazing out toward the window with a smile on his face. He was ecstatic by the call, now having two mercenaries on Dameon's trail.

III

STUDY YOUR ENEMIES

Mason decided to go out for a walk, which has now become a daily exercise. While on his walks, he mediated on such matters concerning himself, his duties, and what could be on the horizon as far as talk amongst the public on his bionic tech. As he walked, he stopped to see someone standing in front of him, wearing a brown leather trench coat and their face was hidden by a hat.

"Why are you in my way?" Dameon asked.

"Because you're the one I've been sent to find."

"Is that right?"

The strange man removed his coat, unveiling his tactical uniform. Militaristic in style, yet very sleek. From his sides arose two machine guns, which he began to fire. Dameon dodged the incoming shots, blocking them with his right arm. Pedestrians nearby ran for cover. The strange man walked toward Dameon, continuing the fire.

"I've been promised a good payday to take you out."

"Tell me, who's paying you?"

"Don't worry about it. Concern yourself with this moment."

The gunfire ceased. The man moved quietly as Dameon ran into the nearby alleyway. The man circled his surroundings, searching for Mason. he chuckled under his breath.

"You know how to move quick. I'll give you that."

"Tell me who hired you?"

"Like I said, don't worry about it!"

The stranger turned around, finding Dameon standing in front of him. Mason delivered a quick blow to the stranger's abdomen, causing him to stumble. Dameon pounced on him, holding him down as he raised his left arm. The arm started to click and its muzzle eased out near the stranger's forehead.

"I'm going to ask you again. Who sent you?"

"If I tell you, will you let me live?"

"Depends on my generosity."

The stranger laughed.

"His name is Aaron Conroy."

"Conroy?" Mason uttered.

"You know him." The stranger said. "Ah, it makes sense now."

"What makes sense?" Mason said, easing off the stranger.

"He came to you already. You declined his offer and now he's sent me and another to follow your trail."

"He sent someone else after me?"

"Aaron is well reserved in resources." The stranger said, standing up. "You wouldn't believe the things he can do."

"Why did he send you after me?"

"To see how you'll react to an instant attack. I saw your ways and I can say, Aaron will be pleased to hear of this."

"Where is he?"

"Don't know. He moves like the winds to various sites. If you want to find him, you'll have to wait for him to approach you. But, you already knew that."

Dameon nodded.

"What's your name?"

"Folks call me the Spymaster."

"I better not see you around here again. Otherwise, I'll blow your head off."

Spymaster grinned.

"I look forward to it. If the call is made."

Spymaster turned, walking away from Dameon. As he went further, Mason thought to himself of Spymaster's words and walked in the opposite direction. Yet, while all this was ongoing, Penalty stood atop a rooftop nearby and observed the scene. From visual to audio recording. Penalty was learning more and more about Mason and what he is capable of.

Nathan worked at his desk, reading up on more files pertaining to Mason and how the law will attest to his actions. He heard a knock at the door and in came Aaron Conroy. Startled Nathan for a moment, being unaware of such a visitor.

"I'm sorry to bother you, Mr. Armstrong." Conroy said. "But, I was the one who called for a meeting."

"I see. Why didn't you give a name?"

"To keep my footsteps discreet."

"So, what do you want?"

"What I want is simple. Nothing big. I want the bionic tech from that Dameon guy."

"You mean his bionic limbs?"

"Yes. What else is bionic on him? Don't answer that."

"I'm not sure I can help you with that."

"But, you can. Because I know of your history. Before all of this law firm junk."

"Have you been following me?"

"No. I'm not a stalker. I like to research those who I seek to do business with. And, what I found about you, goes right into my favor."

"And what is in your favor?"

"Your other occupation."

"What of it?"

"You have 'options' to make things happen. I would like

something to happen in a short amount of time.”

"What if I decline your offer?”

"You don't want to find out.”

IV

<u>**FIRST STRIKE**</u>

Dameon, Brad, and Claire were out in Grant Circus Park, taking a walk. Dameon wanted to clear his head after his confrontation with Spymaster while Brad and Claire wanted to speak with him concerning his actions as a hero. Although, Dameon already stated he's not a hero.

"You can do a lot more." Brad said.

"And what will it cost?"

"Cost?"

"If I was to go out and 'save' people, what would that bring upon me? What if someone was tracking me, they'll lead to you and to Claire. I can't risk that."

"We can take care of ourselves." Claire stated. "No need to worry about us."

"Like how you were inside that warehouse with Vargas and his assassin."

"That's different, Dameon."

"No. It's the same. You know it and I know it."

"Just take some thought on it."

"I've done enough thinking. I'll do what is necessary."

While they continued their walk, a bullet grazed a tree right in front of Dameon. He caught the sound and immediately told Brad and Claire to leave the scene. More shots fired near his location as civilians noticed something going on. Dameon moved through the trees as more rounds were fired. One at a time. Dameon ran over, ducking on the side of a fountain, he looked up and with his bionic enhancements, he was able to scan the nearby buildings. Atop one was a man with a rifle. He had his eyes set on Dameon. His finger was on the trigger. He was set to fire and Dameon took off. Penalty removed his finger and sighed.

"He's clever. Skillful. Useful."

Dameon arrived back at his home where Brad and Claire were waiting inside. Upon Dameon arriving, he found a visitor was also present in the home. Sitting in a seat opposite of Brad and Claire who were on the couch.

"The hell are you doing here?" Dameon asked.

"I came for a reason." Nathan Hawke said. "Just here me out."

"You let him in?" Dameon asked Brad.

"He said he had something important to share with you. Concerning your status."

"Status? This man doesn't tell me anything."

"I know what you've been through."

"Do you?"

"You're not the only one who had to be filed with bio-nanotechnology in order to survive a disaster."

"You still have your legs. Your arms. You don't have to live every day with a bionic reactor in your chest. Embedded through your skin."

"I do not."

"Then, you do not understand what I have to live with!"

"Perhaps not. But, I come here to offer you an opportunity to make things right."

"What kind of opportunity?"

"Join us. Join the Resistance. You've helped us in the Battle of Retropolis and against that King Stroh Conqueror guy."

"I can't accept."

"Why not? You have the qualities of a hero."

"I'm just a soldier. Always will be."

Nathan nodded. "Contact me when you change your mind."

"And what if I refuse completely?"

"Trust me, this isn't our last encounter."

Hawke walked toward the door and left. Dameon focused his sights on Brad and Clare who approached him from the couch.

"Why did you turn him down?" Brad asked.

"Because I don't trust him."

Elsewhere, Aaron met up with Penalty in an undisclosed location. Penalty handed him the data pertaining to Dameon's movements and skill set. Aaron was impressed and knew Penalty was the right guy for the task.

"This man cannot be tampered with." Penalty said.

"Tampered? What do you mean by that?"

"He's an angry man. Even when he appears calm. Anger is sitting right underneath his façade. At a split moment, he can snap and unleash the fullness of his biotech."

"So, what are you proposing I do?"

"Leave the Bionic Rage to me. I'll handle him clean."

Aaron nodded with a grin. "I'll leave you to it."

Dameon rested in his home. Asleep. Although within his sleep was not much rest. For within the dream itself were the echoes of gunfire, commands of soldiers, multiple footsteps. Missiles launching from distances. Shouting from commanding officers. Dameon was dreaming of the past. Of the Republic War. Dameon moved with a fierce focus, shooting the opposing soldiers in his sight. Taking them down with every weapon in his arsenal. From an M4 to a shotgun to even his bare hands. Dameon was a ruthless soldier and the war needed soldiers like him. Those who could complete the mission.

V

WITNESSING THE MONEYMAN

The following day, Dameon is visited at his home by Armstrong. Caught off guard by the lawyer's visit, Dameon allowed him inside.

"Why have you come?"

"To give you some news."

"News?"

"Not what you're expecting. Doesn't concern your appearance in the public."

"Then, tell me why you've come to my home."

"I was visited by Aaron Conroy."

"I know him."

"He came to give me a proposition regarding your bionic limbs."

"He already gave me his deal. I turned him down."

"And in you doing so, he has sent mercenaries to track you down and eliminate you. Have you been ambushed or attacked recently since your conversation with Conroy?"

"I was confronted by a man who called himself Spymaster. Later, myself, Brad, and Claire were shot at by a sniper."

"Are Claire and Brad alright?"

"They're fine."

"That's good to hear." Armstrong said with a sigh. "Anyhow,

these attacks were perpetrated by Conroy in an effort to obtain your limbs.”

“So, where is he?”

“You mean Conroy? I have no clue where he could be.”

“I’ll find him.”

“Dameon, don’t do anything you’ll regret.”

“Truthfully, what else do I have left to regret.”

Armstrong left the home and Dameon searched throughout Detroit for Conroy. Having no luck, he decided to use his biotech to track down Conroy. The tracking went across all of Detroit, eventually reaching a lead that led him to the same warehouse where he faced Vargas’ assassin.

Dameon reached the warehouse and standing out front was Conroy with three bodyguards. They entered the warehouse and Dameon moved quietly to follow. He reached the doors just as they entered and then, he couldn’t wait no longer. Mason burst through the door, catching the guards off their post. Conroy turned, seeing Dameon.

“What have we here?”

“I know what you’ve been up to.”

“Up to? Like what do you mean?”

“The Spymaster. The sniper. I know you paid them to have me killed so you could take my limbs and my reactor.”

Conroy held his hands up with a laugh.

“Sounds like an interesting plan. But, I have no clue what you’re talking about. I‘m just the moneyman.”

“Cut the shit.”

Conroy nodded. “Fair enough.”

The three guards raised up their firearms and before they could fire, Dameon fired his own shots from his right arm through their heads. Precision was perfect. Conroy was silent as Dameon approached him. Facing him directly.

“You will cease whatever else you have planned. Or else, you have a bullet in your own damn head."

Conroy stared and slightly grinned. Dameon noticed the grin and before he could make a move, a gunshot was fired. Conroy dodged out of the way as another shot was fired. The rounds came from in front of Dameon and walking out of the shadows was Penalty. Conroy began applauding his entrance.

"That's the shit I'm talking about!"

Dameon stumbled in his steps as Penalty inched closer. He grabbed Mason by his throat and threw him out of the window to the outside. There, Penalty jumped from the window, standing above Dameon. Aaron came out from the doorway and saw the two on the ground.

"I'll finish the job." Penalty said to Conroy.

"Already looks like you're done."

"Not yet. He still breathes."

VI

YOUR DATE IS SET

Dameon stood up on his feet, facing Penalty. Their eyes were locked onto one another. Penalty was prepared for the fight while Conroy stood by the entrance door.

"Stanton, what are you waiting for?" Conroy yelled. "Kill him!"

"He paid you to kill me?" Dameon asked.

"He did. Your bionic technology would prove useful to Conroy and his business necessities."

"I don't think they'll do any good in a hand of a businessman."

"I'm a moneyman!"

"And I like money."

Penalty took out two Glocks from his sides and began firing at Mason, who blocked the rounds with his arms and ran for the nearby containers, hiding behind them. Penalty ceased his fire as Conroy walked down the stairs.

"Don't get in the way." Penalty said. "I have him where I want him."

"I just wanted to get a closer look. That's all."

Penalty went over toward the nearby pickup truck, Dameon watched him from the corner of the containers, seeing Stanton lifting a rifle.

"That's what he tried hitting me with."

Penalty set up the rifle and Conroy loved the appearance of it. The sleekness and the presence it carried with it. He pointed toward it with joy, placing his hands over his chest with a smirk.

"Where did you get that beauty?"

"Hard earned jobs provided a way. This one cost big."

Mason dove from the containers, his arms clicked as he fired rounds back at Penalty. He dodged toward the truck and Conroy ran form the area. Dameon walked toward the truck, continuing his firing shots. Penalty counted to three and bolted up from the other side of the truck, kicking Dameon in the face and tripping him with a swipe kick. Dameon flipped himself up to his feet, staring down Penalty.

"You have skills. I like a fighter with skills. It gives a proper challenge."

"If that's the case. Face me like a man. No weapons."

Dameon shook his arms and they clicked, becoming silent. He jerked his wrist as the bullets rained down from his forearms. Penalty nodded, dropping his handguns, and placing the rifle in the back of the truck.

"Your move." Penalty grinned.

The two collided with punches and kicks. Dameon's attacks carried weight due to the bionics. However, Stanton did not stumble from the blows, he took them and fought back with attacks of his own. Using many kicks and chest hits against Rage. One chest attack directly hit the reactor and Dameon began to stumble in his steps.

"Was that too hard of a hit?" Penalty mocked. "If not, keep coming."

Dameon went for a punch, but Stanton dodged. Another punch, this time came from the left arm and Stanton dodged once more. He grabbed the bionic arm and slammed Mason to the concrete. He raised his foot to stomp and Dameon rolled out of its way. He stood up and grabbed Penalty by his heck and threw him against one of the wooden containers. Penalty took a moment to get back up as he was catching his breath.

"Is that all you have?" Dameon mocked back. "If not, keep coming."

Stanton laughed. Nodding and wiping the blood from his mouth as he stood up.

"I see. I take it you're holding back."

"What choice do I have. My limbs could easily kill you."

"Stop being a bitch. Use what you have. Before I go ahead and blow your head off."

Dameon nodded.

"Fair enough. You asked."

Stanton rushed toward Dameon with a gut punch. He reached closer and Rage grabbed his arm, twisting it before head-butting Penalty and throwing him to the ground. He stood over Stanton and began pummeling him. Conroy was afraid and ran over to stop Mason from killing Penalty. Shoving Conroy away, Dameon arose and Stanton was bleeding on the ground. Knocked unconscious. Broken bones were definite. Mason walked over toward Conroy, who was crouched on the ground.

"Don't kill me."

"I'm not going to kill you. Just hear me out."

"What do you want? Money? I can give you money."

"I don't want your money. I want you to leave Detroit. Take anything connected to you and your name out of this city. If not, I will find what you have left and finish what has begun here."

Aaron nodded in fear of Dameon's threat. Mason took one look at the downed Stanton and walked away, leaving Conroy behind with his mercenary.

Sometime later, Armstrong secured a deal for Mason to go out into the public eye once more, but he declined. Brad and Claire continued to assist Mason in any needs he might have, but he chose to only contact them on certain occasions. After some thought, Dameon made a choice. One in which his life will forever be altered. One night, a group of gangs had a meeting in downtown Detroit, discussing terms for the next shipment of drugs and weapons. Before they could finish the deal, Mason entered the room, startling the young men.

"Who the hell are you?"

"I'm the dealer. Your time is up."

"Or what?" One thug said as the others raised their weapons toward Mason.

"I guess you'll have to find out."

Mason raised his arms, revealing them to be enhanced and now firing rounds like an assault rifle. He shot up the entire room, killing both gangs. Mason had become a vengeful soldier. He has finally become the Bionic Rage.

TERROR: KILL OR BE KILLED

I

MARKING THE ORDER

John Terror continued cleaning Chicago of anything related or pertaining to Agency X. He traveled all through the city and even went further out into the state of Illinois to rid it of Agency X. Carl Prater detailed all the known locations and their whereabouts, giving the information to Terror and he would head out and decimate them. Burning down entire warehouses and facilities. Within the city, Jordan Dodson kept tabs on Terror's actions as well as the growing concern of nubreeds and rising heroes being looked at in a negative manner throughout Chicago.

Elsewhere, Professor Mite gathered what he could find and made another Agency X base far from Illinois. Most of the crew came from the same base as before. Mite worked in his lab, similar to the old one. Hunter Vazquez sat next to him at the desk, dressed in the same attire as before. Black trench coat, boots, pants, gloves, and his sunglasses. Mite was detailing a map. The map was of the United States and there were red marks across the map. Each mark was a signified area for Agency X to operate.

"We would've had something in Chicago." Vazquez said.

"But, John, he had to mess things up."

"John is the persistent type." Mite replied. "You know this just as much as I."

"What are we going to do once he finds out what's next? You know he will."

"I'm counting on it and that is why I have you."

"What do you have in mind?"

"I've gathered some students that I would like you to lead."

"Lead?" Vazquez questioned.

"You will meet them soon enough and believe me, when John sees them and you as the lead, he will consider other means of operations."

"I see."

"They should be here at any moment."

"Very well. I will greet them upon their entrance."

Vazquez walked out of the lab as Mite continued focusing on the map. He laughed to himself, shaking his head with a smile.

"John has no idea what he's done."

II

ARMS OF THE AGENCY

Terror returned to his hideout, meeting Carl at the desk, reading a map. Terror removed his coat, placing it on the rack near the door as Carl turned toward him.

"You're back. Great."

"I went around. Searched for anything related to Agency X. burned them all down."

"Just as was planned."

"How's the reporter doing on her end?"

"So far, I've received nothing. But, she is working her hardest on finding out more sources. She's very persistent."

"I am aware." Terror nodded. "Now, what's on the agenda for Chicago's criminal elements?"

"Right now? Nothing."

"Can't be? There's sure to be something taking place."

"Not like before." Prater noted. "After the whole 'risen heroes' thing spread across the country, many crime activities began to slow down. Here in Chicago, they've decreased exponentially. Due to-"

"The Yonderers and myself. Great."

"And that Devil guy."

"Never met him."

"I'm sure we'll all meet soon. Just depends on the case I take it."

"Not something I'm looking forward to. There's already enough wanderers outside to deal with."

"Speaking of wanderers, there's this place in the outskirts of the city. You haven't been there yet, have you?"

Terror walked toward the desk, seeing the map on the computer screen. What he saw was a base. One familiar, yet different.

"I have not. How far out is it?"

"Further out than before." Carl said. "You know where the place is?"

"I do." Terror said, grabbing his coat from the rack. "I'll be back."

The door closed behind Terror. Prater shrugged his shoulders and went back to his work.

Terror rode out to the location and upon inching closer, he could hear the sounds of other vehicles behind him. Terror sighed, slowly turning in toward the entrance of the hidden facility. When he turned, he found himself staring down a team. A team of other nubreeds.

"The hell?" Terror said.

The team standing in front of him were consisted of Professor Mite's recruits. They were Kudo Fox, Mistress Destroyer, Agents 51 and 50, and Hellshot. They were led by Hunter Vazquez, who grinned when Terror saw them.

"Found yourself some new friends?" Terror joked. "Quaint."

"Things have changed." Vazquez said. "What you did before won't cut it any longer. Mite wants you back. Although, I prefer you were just dead."

Terror pushed back his coat, raising up two machine guns. The team held up weapons of their own. Kudo Fox wielded two silver glocks, Mistress Destroyer had claws emitted from her hands, Agents 50 and 51 carried pistols, and Hellshot pulled out a sword and a pistol. Vazquez crouched down, his eyes locked on Terror.

"Let's get this over with." Terror said. "Enough wasting time."

Terror fired the first shot before the others could retaliate. Terror looked over to his right, seeing a large dozer. He ran over to it while firing to get cover. The force behind Mite's team was strong. Vazquez stood back while the others took shots toward Terror. Bullets bouncing off the dozer. Terror held his head down, raising up his right arm to fire back. He continued and paused to reload, hearing the bullets coming from the other end.

"Perhaps you should get closer." Vazquez told the team.

"What about you?" Kudo asked.

"I'll do me, and you do you."

From around the corner, a round of bullets fire off near Vazquez and the team. Vazquez lunged from the incoming rounds like a panther while the team ducked their heads. Vazquez looked over toward the dozer, seeing it was not Terror who fired the shots. He looked around before a grenade landed in front of him and the team.

"Move out!" Vazquez yelled.

The team jumped as the grenade exploded. Terror looked out, seeing an opportunity to move ahead. Terror could hear to sound of an incoming motorcycle to his left. He turned, seeing a woman sitting atop a motorcycle next to his. What caught his attention more so was her fiery red hair and emerald eyes.

"You." Terror said.

"Get on your bike and let's get out of here!"

"You. But, how?"

"I'll explain on the way." She said.

Terror ran and sat atop his bike, starting the engine as Vazquez arose from the ground, watching them.

"Nice to see you again." Terror said.

"Same."

The two rode off. Vazquez stood up, fixing his coat and dusting off his sunglasses. He attempted to run after them. But stopped in his tracks. He turned around toward the Agents, who were already sitting on motorcycles of their own as the engines roared. No emotion on their faces. Vazquez pointed out toward Terror and the woman.

"You know what to do."

The Agents nodded and rode off.

III

<u>WHERE IS YOUR FAITH?</u>

The Agents chased down Terror and Horror through the highway, entering downtown Chicago. Terror looked back, seeing one of the Agents inching closer. He turned toward Jade, nodding his head as she looked back. The Agents reached to their side, raising up their firearms and firing. Terror and Jade dodge the incoming shots by moving across pathways of the road, leading into the opposite lanes.

"Shoot at the tires!" Terror yelled.

Jade pulled out a firearm from her jacket, firing toward the agent behind her with a slight hit at the agent behind Terror. She turned around and quickly maneuvered the motorcycle from the incoming traffic on the opposite lane. Terror did the same, giving them a way to escape the sight of the agents. The agents pulled over to avoid the traffic and looked on, seeing Terror and Jade ride off in the distance.

"We must inform Vazquez." Agent 50 said.

"Not before we talk with the Professor. He might have some alternatives to all of this."

Terror returned to his base, entering to find Jordon Dodson talking with Prater. They noticed Terror enter and Jade behind him. Prater looked toward Jade, pointing heavily as Terror approached him.

"It can't be."

"Don't worry, Carl." Terror said. "It is."

Carl only stared as Terror and Jade passed by. Jade gave him a nod and nervously nodded back.

"Didn't expect to see you again."

"Things change." Jade said. "Hell, circumstances decide our course."

"You could say that." Terror added, looking over to Jordan. "Ms. Dodson, I wasn't expecting you to arrive this day."

"I had to come by to see how things are operating."

"For more publicity or just in the arts of curiosity?"

"You could help with something. Carl, with me."

"Sure."

They followed Terror to his desk, where he moved nearly everything off and placed a map. He marked circles around several locations before placing focus on another. The one afar off from Chicago.

"Professor Mite is continuing his operations here."

"And that's where you went?" Prater asked. "And ran into this woman?"

"She came after. Saved me some trouble of escape."

"I'm sorry." Jordan said toward Jade. "Who are you?"

"I'm Jade."

"Tell her your last name." Carl joked.

"Your last name?" Jordan asked. "Is it something to be funny or?"

"Friends in our inner circle called me Jade Horror."

Carl looked over to Terror, who shook his head in silence.

"She is as furious as they come." Carl said to Jordan. "You wouldn't want to get on her bad side."

"I'm sure."

"She is furious." Terror said. "When the situation calls for it."

"And she's called Horror." Jordan added. "While you're referred to as Terror. What group were the two of you involved into get those names?"

"Past lives." Terror replied. "Nothing more to it than that."

Jade cocked her head with a nod.

"Right about that."

"So, what's the current status on Agency X?" Carl asked.

"They're still in Illinois. Far out from Chicago's limits. Mite has a new team of nubreeds besides Vazquez and Agent 51. I recognized two of them from General Rilla's Fellowship."

"Are we going to jump the place?"

"No. I need to meet with an old mentor. Someone who might have some answers."

"I don't know anyone of that nature, John. Much less someone of an old stature."

"But we do." Jade said. "You want to meet with Father Reynolds, don't you?"

"He's familiar with all of this. He might know something we don't."

"I see."

"We're coming with you." Carl said. Grabbing his coat from the rack on the wall.

"No." Terror replied quickly. "You and Jordan stay here. Keep doing what you're doing. Jade and I will meet with Father Reynolds."

"Oh." Carl said, placing his coat back. "I got you."

Terror and Jade arrived at St. Peter's Catholic Church. Jade stood in front of the building while Terror walked and stood next to her, looking at the imagery of Christ upon the cross. Jade looked at Terror with a smirk.

"Still bothers you?" Jade asked.

"I've gotten over it."

"We'll see."

The two entered the church and once they were inside, they walked down the aisle. No one was sitting at the pews but standing in front speaking with someone was Father Scott Reynolds. While talking to the visitor, Scott looked out, seeing Terror and Jade approaching. He nodded and finished up his talk. Once the visitor left, Scott greeted Terror and Jade with hugs.

"I wasn't expecting either of you to be here in a place like this."

"We didn't come by for a simple visit."

"Then, why have you come to see me? What's happened?"

"The Agency still exists." Terror said. "They're operating in the outskirts of city currently."

"Agency X is what you're speaking of?"

"Yes." Jade replied. "We figured we'd come and see what directions you could give us."

"Why me?"

"Because you helped us the last time. Figured you could assist us again."

"Now, I would love to help, but, I'm in no fighting condition any longer."

"We're not asking you to fight with us physically. More so spiritually."

"I can sense you're still delving into those occult reigns."

"He still has the marks to prove it." Jade said.

"They can't be removed. I've tried everything. But, that's not why we're here."

Scott nodded with a smile. He thought to himself for a slight second before returning his senses toward Terror and Jade. Scott rubbed his hands together and clapped.

"I'll see what I can do."

"Thank you." Terror replied, extending his hand.

Scott looked at Terror's hand and shook his head. Going in for another hug. Afterwards, Terror and Jade made their way to leave.

"One more thing, John." Scott said. "Since you stepped foot in here, you realize they're going to send one on your trail."

Terror thought and he understood Scott's words. Terror shrugged his shoulders and his arms flopped up and back down. Not a care in his presence.

"Let them come."

Terror and Jade exited the church. Outside the church, the two talked of possible scenario once returning to the Agency's base. Terror proclaimed to Jade that Carl and Jordan might have to accompany them, but, as it is with Terror, he prefers to go at it alone. However, with Jade at his side, it gives him a better advantage. Jade returned to the base while Terror went out scouting for any more clues leading to the Agency. On the way, Terror encountered a peculiar and macabre figure. Terror found himself in an alleyway within downtown Chicago, staring down the figure.

"The hell are you?"

Terror noticed the clothing the figure wore. It was his own but burnt to crisp with fragments of leather flaking off as the figure walked slowly. Other signs upon the clothing were dried blood. Terror looked at the figure's chest and saw his insignia upon it, only upside down and darkened as if it was submerged in smoke and ash. The figure's eyes were covered by burned sunglasses.

"You're me." Terror said. "From another time or place."

The figure screeched at Terror, lunging at him with both arms grabbing Terror's coat. Terror fought off the figure with kicks and some punches to the face, breaking its sunglasses and revealing its eyes. They were black and only black. No pupils.

"Ah. I know what you are." Terror said, shoving the figure back. "You're a doppelganger of mine. From the spiritual realm. I wonder what they call you."

The figure ran toward Terror once more, finding itself at the barrel of a shotgun, which Terror fired, and the figure vanished in a thick puff of burning smoke with only ash remaining on the ground. The gun's sound echoed through the alley and into the streets, leaving Terror to only run from the scene as quickly as possible. Terror done so and returned to the base.

IV

<u>FINAL BLOW</u>

When Terror had returned, Jade already informed Prater and Jordan on the current circumstances and told them they could join in. Terror approached them, hearing the conversation.

"Better it's just the two of us." Terror said.

"We could distract them." Carl noted. "I mean, we can do things."

"This is not something simple. Last we saw, there were six of them. They're all nubreeds. No human can match them in slight skills."

"But, you and Jade can handle them because your of the same kind." Jordan said. "Makes sense."

Terror nodded and turned toward Jade. The two gathered whatever weapons they needed from the armory. Before leaving, Carl handed Terror a small, but fragile grenade. Terror looked at it as just a simple grenade, however, Carl proscribed him to use it at the opportune time when inside the Agency building. Terror agreed and left the base.

Once Terror and Jade arrived at the Agency base, they saw Vazquez and Mistress Destroyer standing at the front, watching them closely. They stepped from their motorcycles and approached Mite's team a few feet. Terror looked around, not seeing the Agents nor the others who were present the time before.

"Where are the others?" Terror asked.

"They're on some other business." Vazquez said. "What does it matter to you?"

"Nothing. Just gives us a better chance."

Vazquez removed his trench coat and balled his hands up. Mistress Destroyer screeched with a loud yell as her fingers curved sharp. Jade saw the transformation and nodded with a slight clap.

"Not bad. Didn't know she had those."

"Let's go ahead and finish this." Vazquez said, running toward Terror.

"Sure." Terror replied, removing his coat and tossing his sunglasses.

Terror and Vazquez clashed with fists to face. Jade and Destroyer moved swiftly across the field with Jade dodging Destroyer's claws. Terror didn't bother to use his firearms and instead focused on his fists and feet against Vazquez. This time, Vazquez had the upper hand on Terror, grabbing him by his throat and slamming him into the dirt. Terror flipped himself to his feet and continued fighting. Using jabs against Vazquez's lower back and abdomen while using an uppercut against Vazquez's jaw.

"You're stumbling." Terror sighed. "I have you again."

"This will not happen again."

"Looks like it is."

Jade dodged more of Destroyer's swipes before kicking her in the knee to gain a swift uppercut, knocking Destroyer back several steps before Jade speared her to the ground, pummeling the woman until she was unconscious. Jade sighed, looking up toward Terror and Vazquez.

"Finish it, John."

Vazquez punched Terror several times in the chest and face. Terror attacked back with the same hits. They circled one another before Jade ran in, snatching the grenade from Terror's coat and tossing it into the window of the base.

"Let's get out of here!" Jade yelled.

Terror and Jade ran to their motorcycles as the grenade exploded, knocking Vazquez forward into a nearby ditch and covering Destroyer with debris. The base was destroyed as flames covered the grounds, Terror put on his sunglasses as they rode away. A few hours later, Mite returned to the base, seeing its destruction. He sighed before turning around to see a wounded Vazquez and a burnt Destroyer.

"He did this." Mite said. "I already know. Good thing, I have many contingences."

A few days later, Terror spoke with Carl, Jordan, and Jade at the base concerning more possible Agency bases. A knock came from the door and Carl answered, seeing Professor Cullen Edge. He entered the base and Terror greeted him, yet with caution.

"Why have you come here, Professor?"

"I need your help. Both of you." The Professor said, looking at both Terror and Jade.

"Our help for what reason?" Jade wondered. "What's happened?"

"Trouble for pour kind as arisen. We need all we can to fight back. Will you join us on this cause?"

"Let's see what we're up against." Terror replied.

Q-ARROW: HIRED FOR ARROW

I

THE CALL

In the outskirts of Las Vegas, the Hitman was settled at a secure ranch. The ranch was bought by Hitman due to his occupation. Inside of the home, he sat down at a desk, reading up on the news surrounding the risen heroes. Turning the pages, he came across what went on in Vegas concerning Q-Arrow and Woodstalker.

"You've got to be shitting me." He scoffed.

He turned the page and read how the city was greeting Q-Arrow as their own risen hero amongst the others. The Hitman tossed the pages aside and sat still. Meditating and moving through his own thoughts. How could he get back at Q-Arrow after their last encounter? How can he get back into Vegas while being on their watch list? After some time of thinking, the phone rang. He looked and answered it without hesitation as if he was anticipating a call of some sort.

"Yes."

"Is this John Samuels?" A voice said on the other end.

"It is. Who's calling to know?"

"We have a job for you."

"What is this job?"

"You want another chance at Q-Arrow?"

"I do."

"This is that job."

"And what must I do?"

"Kill the son of a bitch. We have the eliminate him to move further our plans."

"I see. Where can we discuss terms?"

"We know you're a hot one in Vegas, but, we can make things for the better. Come into the city by nightfall, we'll meet up and I'll explain everything there. Good?"

"Good."

Later in the night, Hitman made his arrival in Vegas secretly. Upon entering, he is greeted by a black SUV and standing by are two guards in suits with no ties. Hitman nodded as he stepped forward. The guards were quiet. Discreet. The windows of the vehicle were heavily tinted.

"This must be it."

One guard opened the car door and Hitman entered. After the door shut, he saw himself sitting in front of the man who called him. He was a well-dressed man and middle-aged. However, Hitman had no clue who this man could be or who he worked with or for.

"You are the Hitman."

"I am. I take it you're the one who called."

"That I am. Good for us to meet in person. Now, would you like to hear about the offer?"

"Most certainly."

"Very well. Q-Arrow has caused a rift in our operations for this city. His actions violate everything we stand for. Now, we could handle matters ourselves, but it would be too sloppy. However, we received word about your previous encounter with the man. Knowing full well you want some payback."

"That I do."

"This job is your opportunity."

"You want me to kill Q-Arrow and?"

"And the task will be done. He'll be out of our way. You get your payback. All's well."

"Who are you?"

"You'll find out with the rest of the city."

The car door opened for Hitman to exit, but before he could, the man placed his hand on his shoulder.

"I would move with speed if I were you. Because, there are three others seeking to do the same task."

"Three others?" Hitman questioned. "Who are they?"

"You'll find out. I'm sure you'll all bump into each other on this."

Hitman nodded and exit the car, returning to his own and leaving the city.

II

THE BOUNTY AND THE HUNTED

During the same night, Q-Arrow patrolled Las Vegas, searching for any trace leading to the Hitman. Throughout the night, there was nothing Q-Arrow could find that would bring him to the Hitman. Q-Arrow sighed and returned to his lair. As he was leaving, there were three figures watching him closely.

Back at the base, Karen entered, and Jarvis approached her. She looked around for Asher, seeing he was not there.

"Where is he now?"

"He's on business. He'll be back when he comes back."

"Business. You mean out riding about with his archery gear."

Jarvis scoffed. "Give it time."

"He knows he can get himself killed out there."

"He's been through a lot in this short time. He has the experience capable of taking care of himself out there."

"Just because he helped a bunch of strange people in another country doesn't mean he can fully protect himself."

"He's found an ally in the field."

"An ally?"

"He'll be fine. You can wait here until he returns, or you can leave. Your choice."

Karen shook her head, giving Jarvis a look of certainty.

"I'll be back."

Karen left the base as Jarvis went back to his work.

Elsewhere, Jeff Nero was training at his residence, he kept bringing up the events concerning Woodstalker and the Dominate Trio to keep his mind focused. On the other end, he remembered all Q-Arrow told him. While training, he had his cell phone on standby. Waiting for the call to assist Q-Arrow once again.

Deep in Vegas, Q-Arrow discovered a set of tire tracks. Scanning them, he concludes the vehicle appeared from outside the city. He searched every perimeter of the area. Finding nothing that could lead him to the Hitman. Arrow contacted Jarvis and gave him the details. Q-Arrow looked up, seeing a set of cameras.

"Check the cameras of the street." Arrow said.

Jarvis went to the desk of the base, going into the city's camera network. Searching through and searching, Jarvis found the street and went into the camera's history. On the screen appeared the SUV and approaching the vehicle was the Hitman.

"An SUV was there." Jarvis said.

"What of Hitman? Was he present?"

"He was. However, he did not get out of the car. He went inside."

"I'm not clearly getting what you're saying."

"What I'm saying is the Hitman was only a guest to the one inside the vehicle."

"You're thinking what I'm thinking?" Arrow asked.

"I am, sir. There's a bounty on your head."

The crashing jolt of a falling trash can sound off behind Arrow. He turned around as Jarvis tried to get his attention. He held his bow up and the arrow was ready to fire. What he was looking at were three figures. One gave off the slithering sound of a rattlesnake. The second one resembled the physical feats of a Komodo dragon. The third appeared to have makeshift wings and the beak of a eagle.

"The hell is this?" Arrow said.

"What's going on?" Jarvis asked. "What has your attention?"

"Three people. I'm assuming their people."

"What do you mean?"

"They look like animals."

"Animals?"

The rattlesnake one approached Arrow, revealing itself completely. Standing upright, covered in snakeskin with a the head and tail of a snake. Yet, with arms and legs of a human. Arrow stepped back, his hand tightly gripped the bow.

"The hell are you?"

"I am new to this city. As are my allies."

The others present themselves. Both in similar fashion to the rattlesnake figure. Arrow was at a loss for words. Aiming tightly toward the rattlesnake as his eyes glanced the Komodo and the eagle.

"We have been contacted to find you."

"Find me? For what cause?"

"You seek the one called the Hitman."

"I do. You know him? He's your boss?"

"He's a partner in this endeavor. There's a high price on your head."

"That a fact? How much?"

"Money is not what we're after. We seek only a game. A game of chase."

"Hitman wants the money while the three of you want to chase? For sport."

"It is our nature."

Arrow nodded with a smirk.

"Here's mine."

Without a catch of the eye, Arrow began firing toward the three beings consecutively. They took off, dodging around the corners of the nearby buildings as Arrow made his escape, vanishing from their sights. They came out into the open, seeing Arrow was gone.

"Don't worry. We'll see him again."

Making his move, Arrow is almost hit by a gunshot. He turned around, seeing where the bullet had come and he saw in the distance, Hitman himself with a rifle. Arrow fired toward him, only hitting the side of the window where the Hitman was standing.

"Nice shot!" Hitman yelled. "My turn."

The Hitman fired more rounds as Arrow dodged the bullets and evaded Hitman's sights. Running into a shadowy mist of smoke. While making his move, he appeared across Jeff, who was out on a night walk.

"Q-Arrow." Jeff said.

"Why are you out here?"

"I can say the same for yourself. You seem to be in a hurry."

"There's no time. We need to go. Back to the base."

"I'll follow your lead."

III

THE HIDDEN AND THE TIME

Q-Arrow and Jeff made their moves quickly to avoid the Hitman's coming rounds from the air and the three animal beings on the ground. While running, a spew of venom collapsed on the ground in front of them. They both paused, hearing the rattling behind them.

"What is that?" Jeff said, seeing the three figures.

"That's what I'm trying to figure out."

The figures stared and growled toward Arrow and Nero. The bow was up once again, hearing another faint sound from Hitman's sniper.

"You go where you need to." Jeff said to Arrow. "I'll deal with them."

"I'm not leaving you here against three others."

"Not to worry. I've been training. If you're heading where I think you are, I'll meet you there."

Arrow nodded and left. Jeff faced the three figures.

"Do you guys have any names or are you just simple animals?"

"I am Rattler. This one is Eaglestruck and he is the Ultimate Komodo."

"Just animals then." Jeff scoffed. "Figured as much."

Nero rushed toward the three, using his training to gain a greater advantage. Meanwhile, Arrow returned to the lair, seeing

Jarvis and Arwin sitting inside talking. He quickly entered and caught his breath.

"You're in a rush." Jarvis said.

"The Hitman was on me. Sniper rifle."

"Same Hitman as before?" Arwin asked. "Thought he was done with."

"Not quite."

"What of those things you saw out there?"

"They're animal/human hybrids." Asher said. "Never seen anything like them before. Ever."

"Where are they now?"

"Nero is dealing with them. He'll be here as soon as they're out of his reach."

"You left him out there alone?" Jarvis asked. "Why?"

"Because, the boy is capable. He already knows it. Gave me the chance to escape Hitman's shots."

"Well, what of these animal creatures and the Hitman?" Arwin asked with curiosity. "What is all of this about?"

"The snake said there was a bounty on my head."

"Snake?" Jarvis said. "A talking snake."

"It's not the first one." Arwin noted.

"One had the appearance of a snake. A rattlesnake that is. The other two were of an eagle and a Komodo dragon."

"Where did these things come from?" Jarvis wondered. "This world is turning stranger every day."

"Well, it's always been strange." Arwin said. "It just had to present itself."

Jarvis shook his head after hearing Arwin's response. Asher didn't concern himself with the dialogue and went to the computers, searching throughout the city's camera feeds to track down Hitman and the hybrids.

"You only caught the vehicle?" Asher asked.

"That is all."

Asher nodded, looking at the monitor.

"Once Jeff is with us, we'll come up with a plan. End all of this before the sun rises."

"Wait, you plan on going back out there?" Arwin questioned. "I mean, I know you can handle the battles, but, it's three against one."

"Three against two. Jeff's learning."

"Jeff? Who's Jeff?"

"The young protégé of Asher's." Jarvis said. "They met up during the whole Woodstalker and Trio incident."

"Ah. I see. So, he's an archer as well?"

"More of a fighter than a shooter." Asher noted. "Close combat. Less range."

"I see. Well, I'll be getting back to what I was working on while you wait on your apprentice."

"He's not my apprentice." Asher said. "He's an ally."

"By the way, Karen was here earlier."

"What did she want?"

"She wanted to see you. To see how you're doing."

"That's great. Where did she go?"

"She didn't want to sit and wait here for you. Said she'll be back some other time."

Asher nodded. "That's good. Because the distraction isn't needed right now."

They waited several more minutes and from the door appeared Jeff. Rushing in with tiredness as he collapsed to the floor. Asher and Jarvis helped him up, bringing him to the table. There, he caught his breath and sat still.

"I can see you were clearly hit." Jarvis said, seeing the cuts on Jeff's arms, back, and chest.

"It was for the cause. I dealt with them as best I could."

"They're still out there?" Asher asked.

"Yeah. They didn't follow me. They only said they want you."

"Then, they'll have me."

Asher grabbed his bow and loaded the quiver. He approached the door and stopped. He turned toward Jarvis.

"I'll need the car."

"Of course, you do."

Jeff stood up from the table. "I'm coming too."

"No, you've done enough."

"Let me help out. Just in case they try some distraction. I can be the defense."

"Can you take another hit?"

"I can take a few more. Sure."

"Then, get in the car."

Behind them, Jarvis pulled up in a black and gold vehicle. Resembling a Lamborghini, but clearly used for stealth purposes across short distances. Asher and Jeff entered the car as the engine roared.

"What is this car called?" Jeff asked.

"Haven't thought of a name yet."

"Best you take care of this." Jarvis said. "Arwin worked hard on it."

"It'll come out well."

The car roared once more as it drove from the base and out into the roads.

IV

THE REWARD

Q-Arrow and Nero entered Las Vegas, driving pass the Vegas Strip, seeing the crowds of people staring at the vehicle. Some cheered. Others were silent with astonishment. Never seeing a vehicle such as one before in their presence.

"Why drive into the city?" Jeff asked.

"Because, knowing how the Hitman operates, he'll be easy to track."

"Not understanding how?"

"Because of the people. He's only here for me. Which means he'll be watching me. Tracking me. With the crowd, it'll make things slightly difficult for him."

"And of the hybrids?"

"They'll follow him. Probably lurk around the area. Best to be prepared."

The car stopped as Arrow and Jeff exited to the applause and cheers from the civilians. They did not mind them as immediately, the Hybrids appeared before them, terrifying the crowds into a running frenzy. Just as Arrow wanted. Causing the disturbance, the Hitman was already there, moving through the rushing crowd. Slowing him down. Arrow looked back, seeing the Hitman and smirked.

"Gotcha."

Arrow quickly pulled the bow and fired an arrow, hitting the Hitman in his left shoulder. He jolted from the strike, stopping in his tracks. Arrow yelled to Jeff and Jeff took out several small blades, throwing them at the Hybrids. Stumbling them in their steps. Arrow pulled another arrow and fired it at the feet of the Hybrids, causing an explosion and knocking them to the ground. Arrow ran to the Hitman, hitting him with a tackle. The Hitman rolled over and stood up. Jeff went to run in, but Arrow stopped him.

"Leave him to me."

"What should I do?"

"Watch the Hybrids. Make sure they stay down."

Jeff returned to the Hybrids as Arrow and Hitman circled each other.

"You have a sidekick." Hitman said. "Funny."

"He's not a sidekick. He's an ally."

"An ally. Once I have your head, I'll take his as a bonus."

"We'll find out."

"You don't think this will go for so long do you?"

"Judging by your shoulder, this will be over quick."

"And you know this how? You're no hit man."

"I'm not. But, our skill sets are very similar."

Hitman went for his gun, but Arrow fired a speedy arrow to the Hitman's chest. He paused, dropping the gun as he fell to the ground. Arrow walked over to him. He saw the Hitman was still breathing. He looked over to Jeff, seeing the Hybrids are still down. He nodded.

"That was fast." Jeff said.

"This needed to end this way." Arrow replied.

Several days later, the Hitman and the Hybrids were taken to a secure facility. Asher and Jarvis discovered the ones who Hitman spoke to were an hidden organization. Their purpose was to eliminate the risen heroes across the world. Asher stated he'll speak with a friend concerning the matter. Jeff continued his training, only this time within the base. Karen returned to the base just as Asher was working on some equipment.

"I see you made it." Asher said.

"Figured it was best I come now rather than later."

"So, what did you want to talk about?" Asher asked.

"Your role in all of this."

"What of it?"

"How long will it last?"

"As long as the mission requires it."

I

<u>FIRE</u>

Within the Citadel of Enchantment, Thomas Bradley stood in front of Huang. The two were training in their mystic abilities and feats. Bradley began to conjure mystic energy around his hands and arms, Huang nodded with a smile.

"You're getting better."

Continuing their training, the citadel doors burst open and in came a woman. She was dressed in medieval apparel. Mild chain mail and armor on her shoulders, chest, forearms, and legs. She even wore a tunic and the clothing was a dark violet with white lining. Huang and Bradley paused in their training, seeing the distressed woman.

"Where is he?" She asked.

"I'm sorry, but who are you?" Huang asked.

"I need to speak with him now!"

"With who?"

"Donald! Where are you, Donald?!"

"She's looking for Doctor Fortune." Bradley said.

From the stairs came down Fortune, wearing his sorcerer apparel. He paused at the foot of the steps seeing the woman.

"Morhana."

"I'm sorry to have come uninvited." She said. "I need your help immediately."

"Calm down and tell me exactly why you're here?"

"They're after me."

"Who's after you?"

"The Elemental Gods."

"Elemental Gods?" Huang said. "How can that be?"

"There must be something off." Fortune said. "Are you sure it's the Elementals?"

"I'm positive. They're after me."

"Why would they be after you? You're just a sorceress."

"I can't explain right now."

"You have no other option but to explain."

Before she could utter another word, a large fireball came down from above the citadel, shattering the ceiling, impacting between the four sorcerers, knocking them far from each other. Once the fire settled, Fortune stood up and saw a figure standing where the fireball fell. It looked of a dragon. One standing upright. It had wings and arms.

"There you are." The Dragon said toward Morhana.

"Pardon, you've stepped foot inside my Citadel." Fortune said. "Who are you?"

The Dragon turned toward the Supreme Enchanter.

"You know who I am."

Fortune paused.

"You're the Fire Elemental."

"That I am and I have come for Morhana."

"For what purpose?"

"She has done something unforgivable of our kind. A treacherous act."

Fortune clapped his hands together and from them were summoned mystical energy flames. Huang and Bradley both stood up, prepared to do the same, however Fortune nodded them off.

They stood back. The Fire Elemental stepped forward toward Fortune.

"You seek to harm me?"

"I can't let you hurt Morhana. Or take her anywhere."

"On who's authority?!"

"Mine. You are inside my Citadel. Remember."

The Fire Elemental stood back and released flames from his mouth against Fortune, who guarded himself with the energy around his hands. Fortune began twirling his arms as the energy around him began to cover him, giving him a full shielding. The Fire Elemental continued his blaze as Fortune approached him with one step at a time. Huang wanted to help, but found it best to obey Fortune's command. Bradley watched on as Morhana went and stood next to them. Fortune extended his arms, grabbing hold of the flames and reversed them against the Fire Elemental. The blast pushed the Elemental back at bit as Fortune rushed him and began firing energy bolts from his hands. They resembled golden lightning bolts.

"These tricks won't stop my purpose!"

"I'm not trying to kill you." Fortune said. "I'm slowing you down."

Fortune twists his fingers and beneath the Elemental appeared a portal, wherein remain a pit of flames.

"You seek to send me back to my realm!"

"That's the plan."

Fortune levitated from the ground as the portal started to suck in the Elemental by his feet and tail. He clawed to stay atop the floor as Fortune eyed him from the air.

"This is only the beginning!" The Elemental said. "You sought to help her and now, the others will find you and finish what I've started!"

"Then, so be it." Fortune replied. "By the temporal feats of *Durriken*!"

The portal took in the Fire Elemental and closed. Silence filled the Citadel. Fortune fell to his knees, for he was tired. Morhana walked over to him as did Huang and Bradley.

"Are you alright?" She asked.

"I'll be fine. But, you. You need to tell us everything. Now."

"I... I can't."

"Why not?!"

"Because it's a long, long story."

"We have time. Believe me."

Before she could utter a word, the four of them quickly vanished like a snap of the fingers. They were no longer inside the Citadel. They were somewhere else, and it wasn't on their behalf.

II

<u>ICE</u>

The four sorcerers found themselves somewhere chilly. For the air was cold and beneath their feet laid snow. Fortune looked around, seeing them all to be standing high on a mountain. He looked down and only saw snow and hills.

"What have you done, Morhana?" Fortune asked.

"I didn't do this."

"Where are we?" Huang wondered.

"Far north." Fortune replied. "Very far north."

"I have to ask." Bradley said. "We're not on Mount Everest, are we?"

"We are not." Fortune said. "We're elsewhere. I'm just trying to wonder who would send us here."

"It wasn't me." Morhana said once more. "I had nothing to do with this."

Huang walked around, feeling the cool breeze of wind around them. He closed his eyes, meditating, and as he was, a strange essence came over him. He jumped.

"What's wrong?" Fortune asked.

"We're not alone. Someone else is here. Watching us."

"Who else could be here?" Bradley asked.

Fortune looked over toward Morhana as she slowly started taking steps back near the mountain behind them. He approached her, grabbing her arm tightly. She struggled to get loose, but Fortune's grip was strong.

"Where are you going?"

"Nowhere."

"Why are you trying to hide?!"

"Because, I might know who's here with us."

"Who is it?" Fortune asked. "Tell me now."

Winds picked up around them as they each looked above, seeing a figure coming down from the sky. Upon its landing in their sights, they saw the figure was similar to the Fire Elemental. Yet, this one was made of ice. Pure white body.

"He's found us." Morhana said to herself.

"An ice dragon?" Bradley asked.

"No." Fortune replied. "An ice elemental."

"I guess we'll be helping out this time." Huang said. "I'm ready."

"Bradley, stand back." Fortune said. "Let us handle this one."

"But, master, I can assist in some form."

"I am aware. For right now, we'll deal with this one."

Fortune and Huang stood front, ready to combat the Ice Elemental. It flapped its wings in style, crossing its arms. Glaring at Fortune and Huang, but the focus was all placed on Morhana.

"The witch." The Elemental said. "I've come for you."

"I'm not going anywhere!"

Morhana conjured up a strange, mystical energy dagger, throwing it at the chest of the Ice Elemental. It stepped over and chuckled. Now, rushing itself toward her, Fortune and Huang moved quickly projecting a force field between them and the Elemental. However, the Elemental was not concerned about the sorcerers, but was single-minded on Morhana. Every attack it released was toward her and not Fortune, Huang, or Bradley. Fortune noticed these movements.

"What did you do?"

"I will tell you after we deal with him!" Morhana screamed.

"She has crossed a line only few have dared to scratch!" The Elemental said. "Move aside, sorcerers. Leave this witch to me!"

"I can't do that until I have answers." Fortune said.

Fortune twirled his hands, creating a huge blast of energy, knocking the Elemental into the mountain itself. Huang and Bradley followed with similar, yet minor attacks to slow down the ice figure. Morhana did what she could, but turned to run. Fortune spotted her and grabbed her arm.

"Where are you going?"

"I have to get out of here!"

"You're not going anywhere!"

The Ice Elemental raised its right hand, revealing claws and swiped Huang and Bradley into the mountain and walked toward Morhana and Fortune. Morhana stepped forward and raised her arms, shouting as loud as she could. Fortune also held his hands up. All facing the Ice Elemental.

"You cannot stop one such as I."

The Elemental inhaled as a brightly glow appeared from within its mouth. Ice and snow around the region began to be absorbed into the glow. Fortune looked at Morhana and she done the same. Energy arose from their hands.

"You're ready to talk?" Fortune asked.

"I am."

"Good."

With both their energies focused, they blast the mystic power against the Elemental's ice beam. The forces collide and within the blast, the Ice Elemental backed away, vanishing from their sights. Fortune and Morhana looked around the area, uncertain.

"Where did it go?" Huang asked, getting up from the ground.

"I'm not sure." Fortune said. "Otherwise, it's gone."

Bradley stood up from the ground, looking around through the snowy region. Huang did the same.

"So, that thing just vanished?" Bradley asked.

"Looks to be the case." Huang said.

Fortune approached Morhana with haste.

"Tell us what's going on now."

Morhana nodded with a sigh.

"Ok. I'll tell you. This-"

Without notice they each disappeared from the snowy region and instantly appeared in a vast desert. Huang looked around, seeing the clear sky and nothing but mountains, dirt, and sand around them. The heat of the air was intense and the smell of the ground was noticeable.

"Where are we?" Bradley asked.

"Someplace uncertain." Fortune said. "Morhana, what is happening here?!"

"It's just I did something wrong."

"Tell me now."

III

<u>ROCK</u>

"What did you do?"

"Once again," Morhana said, stepping forward to Fortune. "I didn't do this."

"It appears we're somewhere very far from our previous location." Huang said.

"Is anyone noticing something with all of this?" Bradley asked. "Like, this is designed for a reason."

Fortune took in Bradley's words and turned his attention back to Morhana.

"It's making sense."

"What is?" Morhana said.

"We've defeated the Fire and Ice Elementals and now we're out in some desert land mountains region. You know who's about to show up."

Huang nodded. "A Rock Elemental."

"Yes." Fortune said. "He's coming. Now, Morhana, tell me what's happening."

"I might have done something that humans should not do."

"Such as?"

"I might've-"

The ground began to quake, stumbling the sorcerers in their places. The trembles increased to the point of rocks beginning to fall from the mountains. Fortune placed a force field around himself and the others to avoid the falling debris.

"Prepare yourselves!" Fortune said.

The rocks fell and the quake stopped. As Fortune removed the field, they found themselves staring in the presence of the Rock Elemental. Tall, rugged, made of the minerals of the mountains around them.

"A rock dragon?" Bradley said. "Are they all dragons or something?"

"It's a form they prefer to have when coming upon the earth." Morhana said.

"And you know this how?" Fortune asked.

"Like I said, I'll explain everything. Once we're not interrupted."

The rocky wings flapped on the Elemental as it stood tall. The sorcerers were ready for the fight to come. However, this elemental wasn't seeking a battle with power or might.

"Morhana must come with me."

"I don't believe she will." Fortune said. "She's with us."

"She must explain herself to the others for her crimes."

"Trust me, I am aware."

"Then stand aside, Sorcerer."

Fortune shrugged his shoulders. Holding his hands up with the mystic energy covering them. Huang and Bradley's hands were also held up.

"I cannot do that."

"You take part in her crimes?"

"Truthfully, I do not. I want to know what she's done as well. There's no need for fighting."

"I agreed. I know what the results of my counterparts. They desire combat. However, for one such as I, resolve to speaking terms and now, you say you desire to know the witch's crimes."

"I do."

"Very well. That is the work of another. For I cannot reveal such actions in my wake upon the earth. You must travel into the spiritual dimension to receive the answers you seek."

"You mean you cannot just tell me what she's done?"

"To do so would shake the foundations of the earth. This is not the time for such disturbances."

Fortune looked at Morhana. She stood still.

"Where must we go?" Fortune asked the Elemental.

"To the realm of my other counterpart. The one simply called, '*Ghost*'. you must travel to his realm and all will be revealed."

"And how do we find this realm?"

The Rock Elemental warped his hands and in between them formed a portal. A portal into the dimension of the Ghost Elemental. Fortune examined the portal, seeing its eerie white glow with flashes of an ominous violet light. The sorcerers walk through the portal and it closes itself. Afterwards, the Rock Elemental is gone.

IV

<u>GHOST</u>

The portal flashed and the sorcerers found themselves in the spiritual dimension. Auras of diverse colors surrounded them in every inch. The bright lights within were as bright as the sun, glinting off Fortune's cloak and hair.

"I've never been to this place before." Fortune said.

"Not many have." Morhana added. "But, we're here now."

"Not to fight. To get answers."

Bradley turned to look at the lights and found himself standing in the mere presence of the Elemental that dwells within. The others turned toward Bradley's direction and saw the entity themselves. Wings larger than the others. Its body glared like transparent silver.

"I knew you would come." The Elemental said.

"Good." Fortune said. "Then you know why we're here."

"I do. Because of her actions, you have entered my realm."

"Now, we do not wish to fight. We only want to know what's happening."

"I comprehend your spirits. Unlike my brothers upon the earth, I will tell you why we're after Morhana the Witch."

"Please do." Huang said.

The Elemental warped his hands and the lights around them began to bounce atop one another. Twirling and warping themselves into a mirage. Within the mirage of many colors, Fortune could see the image of Morhana and her actions prior to the visit at the Citadel.

"Why?" Fortune said. "Why did you do it?"

"I had no choice."

"Every being in creation has a choice." The Elemental said. "You made yours and made it poorly."

"I can make things right. Let me make it right."

"How can you?"

"Pardon me, Ghost Elemental, perhaps we can lend a hand to Morhana's actions. Find a way to reverse her doings."

"And how do you perceive to reverse such a transgression?"

"We confront your other brother. The one of the Air."

"I will send you to him now."

Before he could make the way, a bright flash of light emitted from the ground beneath their feet. A sigil of mystic origin appeared and from it arose the Mystic Father. Fortune, Huang, and Bradley bowed in obeisance, Morhana stood by while the Elemental watched in awe.

"The Mystic One."

"Elemental of the Presence."

"Master," Fortune said. "why have you come?"

"To grant you insight on the Elementals and who they truly are."

The Mystic Father gave the Elemental a look of declaration and the Ghost entity nodded.

"They're not just elemental beings. They're gods."

"Gods?" Bradley said. "Not possible."

"It it and they are. Though, not gods of a omnipotent source. They're lesser ones. Created to preserve the elements of creation."

"Why do they appear in the form of dragons?" Huang asked.

"It was the form chosen for the best. Unlike the angels and demons. The Elementals are a peculiar pair of entities."

"We have our duties to uphold."

"Do we all, Ghost God."

The Mystic Father approached Morhana. Slowly and with caution for Morhana's eyes were glowing. The Mystic Father perceived her intentions, placing his hand on her shoulder.

"Stay calm, sorceress. I understand your reasoning."

"Then, you know why I did it?"

"I do. Although, I disagree with it, I understand it."

"What must I do to correct my wrong?"

"Obey the voice of the Ghost God. Whatever he commands you to do, you do."

The previous portal reopen in front of them. Between the sorcerers, Mystic Father, the Ghost God. Winds blew through the portal from within. Huang covered his face with his arms.

"I take it that's above ground."

"It's the only way to meet the Air God." The Mystic Father said. "Ghost God, give them the orders."

"Are you ready?"

"We are." Fortune replied.

"Then jump."

"You will succeed." The Mystic Father told Fortune.

"We'll do our best, master."

Fortune jumped through the portal and the others followed with Morhana stepping last before feeling the glare of the Ghost Elemental. From there, the sorcerers were gone. The Mystic Father stood before the Ghost God.

"We have other matters to discuss."

"Yes, we do." The Ghost God proclaimed.

V

<u>AIR</u>

The sorcerers exit from the portal, finding themselves hovering in the air. Far above ground as the air was slightly thin for their well-being. Bradley took a small look beneath them and couldn't see beyond the clouds.

"What do we do now?" Huang asked.

"We await the Air God." Fortune said. "He's the final one."

In the midst of the air, a whirlwind formed. One of great strength and visibility. Within the whirlwind came out the Air God of the Elementals. Features were the same as its brethren. Although, whiffs of clouds moved through him as if he was indeed solid air.

"I knew you would arrive."

"Good to know." Fortune said. "Then, you know we don't seek to take your time."

"I see the witch is with you. Better the company you destroy than the ones you keep."

"I've never heard that before." Bradley said.

"It's a different spectrum." Huang added.

The Air God hovered before Fortune and Morhana. Looking down at them from its great height.

"We do not seek to fight. As we told your Ghost brother, we, I only needed to know what Morhana has done and I've found out.

Now, I ask of you to forgive her of these stupendous mistakes and grant her a release from the terrors."

"Release? What she done travels far beyond the modern times of humanity."

"If you can't spare her like your brother, then what do you propose?"

"I demand she face her trials."

"But your brother let her go. We could've fought him, but we did not. Instead he opened a portal into your territory. Now, I ask again, what can you do for her safety."

The Air God stared. He turned from them after a slight nod. The sorcerers were unsure as to what the Elemental would say or do. For they waited to hear an answer. After a minute, the Air God turned back to them.

"I will say this. Morhana must not bargain with the natural laws of this world. Nor make agreements with the natural entities. She must not interfere in mortal affairs or affairs pertaining to the earth. Her being a witch, I declare she only remain in the spiritual affairs of this reality. For if she is seen or heard to been active amongst the generations of Man and their activities, she will be hunted down by the spiritual forces which surround us all."

"Do you accept these terms?" Fortune asked Morhana.

Morhana grunted, then she sighed bitterly. "I accept."

"Very well." The Air God said. "Now, go. Return to your Citadel, Donald Fortune. Leave me be."

The Air God waved his hands toward the sorcerers, thereby blasting them from his present and after a second, they found themselves standing inside the Citadel.

"We're back." Bradley said.

"Yes we are." Huang added. "That was quick."

Fortune walked toward the door, he opened it and stepped outside. Morhana followed him as he stood there, looking out at a city in the far distance.

"Thank you."

"No need." Fortune said. "I did what had to be done."

"I guess now I must find something to do. Something in the spiritual fields."

"As do we all."

"What are you implying?"

"This small event has shown me something I've once meditated. I cannot abide in the same presence as those risen heroes out there. It is better for someone like myself to focus clearly on the spiritual matters we have at hand. We must be hidden from the society. We must remain in the shadows of the supernatural. It is our dwelling place."

KULAR THE AQUA-BARBARIAN: LORD OF ATLANTIS

I

<u>DECLARATION</u>

The Kingdom of Atlantis is attacked once again by Lord Shark and his army of the Fanged Ones from the deep. The Atlantean army was ready for their return and the battle commenced on the sea floor. Shark moved with haste through the soldiers in his sights, making way for the palace. Standing at the palace doors was Kular, his trident in hand. Kara, his wife stood by his side, staring out towards the battlefield.

"Are you sure about this?"

"It's my duty as king. Besides, we've been through this fight before. It'll end the same as before."

Kular stormed off toward Shark and his army. With the Atlanteans behind him, all with weapons in hand, they come to a pause as Kular raised his hand. They stopped only ten feet from Shark. Kular stepped forward, staring Shark down.

"Do we really have to go through this once more?"

"You aided the land-dwellers. Giving them the change of studying our domain. You've put us all on the path to extinction."

"I have done no such cause." Kular noted. "I went up there to see how they live. What actions they accomplish as we do here. There was evil up there. But, there was also some good. A balance is in motion in the livings of the land-dwellers. Such as it is in our dwellings."

"Atlantis does not need a king who rallies alongside, grounders. You will face me and my army in war or you can just surrender your crown and ruler ship to me."

"I give you this one offer. Sit with me and we'll discuss this matter between ourselves. Then, after we have our talk, you choose what comes next."

"Sit and talk?! I want you dead and all of those who follow you. For Poseidon's sake, why should I sit at a table with one of your kind?"

"Because this talk is all that's saving you from a quick death."

"You believe so?" Shark said, stepping closer.

"I am." Kular replied. "I could've killed you in our last encounter. I did not. You have life and death standing before you. For your own sake, choose life."

Shark paused himself, yet his eyes were set on Kular. Both armies were ready for the battle. Shark shook himself and sighed.

"Lead the way."

Kular did, leading Shark toward the palace. Upon reaching the steps, Kara saw Shark and was terrified. Novah approached her, cautioning her to be still. Kular looked up toward Novah, seeing Kara's fear in her eyes. Novah nodded and Kular understood. The doors of the meeting room opened with Kular and Shark entering, with only two of their most trusted soldiers. The doors closed as the others looked in.

II

<u>**MEETING OF KINGS**</u>

Kular and Shark sat across from one another with their soldiers standing guard.

"There's nothing to discuss." Shark said. "It's simple. I want this place. This kingdom."

"You can't have it. However, you can go on back to your home and refurbish it into something of this nature."

"Can't do such a thing. All sea-dwellers know the prime capital of the oceans is Atlantis. Hell, if it's not me, the others will come and ry to claim this prize for themselves."

"If that's their desire, we'll be ready for them."

Shark scoffed. "Will you? What of the land-dwellers? What if one of them gets the case of the curious and decides to come down here and invade. It's not unusual."

"From what I learned, there isn't one up there. Not yet anyway."

"Always making such mistakes. You cannot be idle when it comes to them up there. Or those down here."

"I'm not idle. I'm very aware."

"So you say."

Kular stared at Shark with a keen gaze. More so from respect rather than an enemy.

"I'll ask you this one time, will you return to your home and never trespass here again?"

"I'm returning home regardless. But, do not take my leave for a truce. I want this kingdom and I will have it. One day or another."

Shark stood up from the table and left the room with his soldiers. Shark's army left Atlantis and the Atlantean army returned to their duties of the kingdom. Sometime later, Novah visited Kular in his study, seeing him observing a map of the under-kingdoms.

"You understand he will return to claim this kingdom."

"I comprehend well, Novah. However, I will do what is necessary if Shark shall ever step foot on our grounds."

"I must ask, what of the contingences involving the land-dwellers?"

"We will come to those terms when or if a land-dweller seeks to take what is ours."

"Then I take it you already have plans in motion. Just in case."

"That's one reason why I went up there. To not only see how they live and operate. But their skills. Their will. Their focus. There's much good in some of them. We won't have to worry ourselves about them. It is the others who may cause concern in the times ahead. I was told by a eerie one that my future consists of wars. Wars against those of both land and sea."

"An eerie land-dweller?" Novah questioned. "Doesn't sound common."

"He knew more than the common land-dweller. He knew our future. He's seen it."

"And was this dweller benevolent toward you or sinister?"

"Neither. He was what he was."

Novah nodded. Thinking about the dweller, but no image could muster in his mind. He shook his head.

"I will keep my gaze keen on the horizons. Just in case he makes a quick return."

"Thank you."

Novah bowed before Kular and left the study. During the night, Kular went to his chamber, where Kara was waiting. Kular entered the chamber and sighed, not of relief, but of tiredness in mind.

"What do you have planned for Shark's next move?"

"It's under control, Kara. Trust me."

"I know. I know. Just being certain."

III

BATTLES FOUGHT

The following morning, soldiers ran into the palace to alert Kular of a surprise visitor. Kular grabbed his trident and rushed out with them to see what was happening. Upon exiting the palace doors and looking out in the distance, Kular saw Ark, the Sea Monster staring him down.

"Ark." Kular uttered. "I will deal with him alone."

"Are you sure, my king?" A soldier asked. "We can assist you."

"I will be well. Keep guard just in case there are others in the surroundings."

Kular went toward Ark and before he could speak a word, Ark attacked Kular with his claws, swiping and snatching at Kular's armored tunic. Kular fought back with the trident, knocking Ark into the ground with an aerial attack. Kular kicked the Sea Monster back a distance before he could raise himself up onto his tentacle limbs.

"Why are you here?" Kular asked.

"I have to destroy all there is. This kingdom and you."

"So be it.'

Kular swiped the trident across Ark's chest continually until blood flowed from the wounds. Ark stumbled back with his tentacles crushing the ground beneath him. Kular speared the trident into Ark's chest, ramming it further as the monster let out a loud screech. Ark slowed down and Kular pulled the trident from his chest. Ark's head hung low as his body titled over in front of Kular. Kular stepped forward toward Ark, using his foot to see if the monster still lived. Without a second's notice, Ark's head rose up, his eyes dark as the depths of the sea. A big smile formed on his face as he drove his right-handed claw through Kular's chest. The attacked startled all who were watching, including Kara and Novah.

"Is this your king?!" Ark yelled, facing the Atlanteans who were watching.

Ark raised the Aqua-Barbarian over his head and threw him against the palace doors and went off.

"My task is done." Ark said. "I now leave you to your demise."

Kara ran over toward Kular, seeing the blood coming from the wound. The soldiers also stood guard around Kular. Novah looked on, watching Ark leave and within that same distance, Novah caught a glimpse of a coming army. He knew what this all was.

"We have trouble." Novah told Kara and the soldiers, pointing outward.

Kara looked out, stepping further. She saw what Novah saw. An army. Charging toward Atlantis and in front of them was Lord Shark. The sound of the incoming army could be heard from the front of the palace. A sound of a rushing wind buried beneath a solid structure. A faint whistle moving from within.

"This was a set-up." Novah concluded.

IV

WARS CONQUERED

The Atlantean army was prepared and ready for the coming army. Kara tended to Kular, who's wounds continued bleeding. Novah knelt next to him, gazing back and forth between him and Shark's army.

"My lord, Shark is coming with his forces."

"Then, I must…" Kular breathed. "I must protect this kingdom."

"Beloved, you're gravely wounded." Kara noted. "You can't fight Shark in this condition. He'll kill you."

"No, he won't. I will handle this. Very swiftly."

"How swiftly do you intend on ending this?" Novah questioned. "By what power?"

"By the power of the ancients and by the power of Atlantis."

Kular picked himself up, brushing off the assistance of Kara and Novah. He wanted to walk on his own. Holding his chest with one hand and dragging the trident with the other as he stepped down the sapphire steps of the palace and out into the field. He waved the trident toward his soldiers.

"Stand aside. I will take care of this."

"My lord, there's too many of them." A soldier said. "Surely, you will require assistance in this fight."

"I have all the assistance I need." Kular said, holding the

trident. "Now go and keep the kingdom protected."

The soldiers obeyed their king and retreated back to the palace where they stood and watched. Kular moved slow, dragging his left foot while approaching Shark and his army. Kular stopped and held himself up with the trident. Shark and his army made their approach, halting in their steps.

"You're wounded, Aqua-Barbarian."

"No thanks to your diversion."

"Hmm. It seems Ark did a number on you and yet, just in time for us to pick up the pieces."

"Pick up the pieces? That's what you believe this is? How come you couldn't do this on your own? Instead, you bribed the Sea Monster into doing the work for you."

"What's done is done! This kingdom will be mine and your head will be on a pike for all the kingdoms of the seas to witness."

"I think not."

Kular slammed and twirled the trident, conjuring a whirlwind from above, which gathered up Shark's army, scattering them across the distances of the sands. Shark was astounded by the power he witnessed. The water blowing across his face like the winds of the lands. Kular continually twirled the trident. His eyes were set on Shark as he ran toward Kular with his gnawing teeth, a bolt of lightning stroke from the whirlwind, colliding with Shark's chest. Shark fell to the sands, holding his chest in pain. He looked up at Kular, seeing the lightning circling itself around the trident and Kular's hands.

"What power is this?!"

"The power by the ruler of Atlantis." Kular replied. "You're done here."

Kular swiped the trident across the sands and the whirlwind picked up Shark, slamming his sharp hands into the dirt to keep a grip. The might of the whirlwind was very strong as it picked Shark up, tossing him far from Atlantis. The battle was over and

Kular collapsed on the ground. The soldiers went and gathered him up, carrying him to his chambers of the palace. The doctors of Atlantis tented to his chest wounds. After some time, they concluded Kular would be healed within mere days and he will live.

After those days had passed, Kular was up and ruling the kingdom once more. Although, word of his actions have reached the other kingdoms of the seas. Novah came to him in his study and spoke of several armies making their way toward Atlantis. Kular asked if Shark's army was one and Novah declined.

"Then who is it?" Kular asked.

"Sea-Stormers." Novah said.

"Not possible. I killed the Sea Kaiser."

"Well, it appears the Stormers have a new leader and there are others who are on their way."

"Very well." Kular said. "We must prepare."

"Indeed."

DESTINY OF THE CHAMPIONS: THIRST

I

<u>SIGNAL LOCKED</u>

The Spellvector moved through the Time Dimension as the newly formed team sat inside. Doctor Omega piloted as he always does. Jetlash sat next to him, learning about the dimension and how the Spellvector works within the spectrums of time and space.

"You desire to pilot this ship, I see."

"I'm just fascinated that such a ship exists. I am curious as to how it works in full. How does it go from different time periods and this dimension we're in, how does it truly exists?"

"There are many things in the universe that most are not aware of, Corbin. But, you are and this team I've assembled. Together, we can make things better. Protect history as the way it remains."

"What if something goes wrong? We have this ship. We could go back in time and fix what went wrong."

"I advise against it. The comebacks of such an action would bring down much wrath upon anyone who volunteered."

"I assume Baron Eon is seeking to do something like that? Change something in time?"

"He wants to rewrite it completely. Make everything to his liking. In his image."

The radar started to beep as Amadeus looked at the source,

discovering its stronger signal and otherworldly energy emitting from the location.

"I think we've found it."

"Found the box?"

"Yes."

"Where is it?"

"Romania. Present day."

II

<u>A VISITOR UNSEEN</u>

Doctor Omega gathered the team together, comprised of the members before. Corbin Beval, known as Jetlash, Sandra Banks, referred to as Ms. Titan, and Anthony Carlos, called the Crimson Mask. Omega informed them of the whereabouts of the Cosmicbox and how it's apparently sitting in Present Day Romania. Sandra turned to see the map and pointed toward the connected city.

"Bucharest?"

"Precisely." Amadeus said. "We head there now, find the box and retrieve it before Baron Eon discovers us."

"When do we head out?" Anthony asked.

"Right at this moment."

The team sat in their seats as Omega charted the ship toward the Modern-day time strip. In doing so, the ship vanished from the time dimension and appeared in present-day Bucharest. The ship hovered over the city, seeing how the gray clouds to cover the ship from the eyes below. The team teleported to the ground and began walking the streets. Omega pulled out a device from his coat pocket, signaling the source of the box.

"It's near."

They walked continues, following the signal. Once they reached the location, they found themselves in the Old Town district. As they stood, looking around, a woman approached them.

"Great. You guys again."

"You!" Corbin said.

"Calm yourself, Corbin." Amadeus said. "It seems this is the one responsible for thwarting our chance at retrieving the box."

"My name's Tessa Balthazar, in case you've forgotten, I've come to this city to find the box myself."

"Any luck?"

"None. My contact informed me of the Baron in position of the box somewhere in this city. I don't know where."

"We're tracking the box and this device claims the box is somewhere in this Old Town."

"Perhaps I'll find it first."

"Don't pick a fight with us, Ms. Balthazar." Amadeus said. "We don't want any trouble."

"Trouble is my living, Doctor."

Tessa walked away from the Champions, going about her way. Amadeus turned and looked at the device. The signal went quiet and disappeared from the radar. The clouds above them began to grow darker as raindrops started to fall. The device beeped once more, only at this moment there were more than one signal. Seven to be accurate. Omega wasn't sure what they were and during his thinking, the group was ambushed by a quick strike. They stood together as the rain fell heavily, blinding their eyes to the attacker. The strike came at them again, slashing Corbin's sleeve.

"What is that?!"

"I'm not sure." Amadeus said. "But, I've heard of these things before."

The attackers formed a line around the Champions as the rain ceased. Amadeus saw them. Dressed in lean robes with hoods. Their eyes glaring like a fire. Their teeth sharp and inhuman. Amadeus recognized what they were without question. The rest of the team were uncertain, begging to know who they're staring down. Amadeus pointed carefully toward the seven beings.

"Vampires." Amadeus said.

The vampires swarmed around the team. Not attacking, only seeking to frighten them. Amadeus kept the group calm as they already were. One vampire stopped swarming and approached Amadeus. From the look in his eyes and the keen expression on his face, this vampire was not a simpleton.

"You must be Amadeus Omega."

"I am. Who's asking?"

"We have been sent out here to command you and your team to cease from retrieving the Cosmicbox."

"Under who's orders? Eon?"

"Not exactly. Our queen doesn't like it when uninvited visitors invade her dwelling places."

"Your queen?" Corbin asked.

"What's her name?" Sandra wondered. "Tell us please."

"Bathory." The vampire said.

"Bathory?" Amadeus uttered. "You speak of the blood Countess?"

The vampire grinned. "There is only one."

"We would like to speak with her. We need that Cosmicbox back."

The vampire shook his finger.

"The Countess speaks to you when she desires it. She only sends out a warning. Leave. Do not come back."

Anthony stepped up to the vampire. He wore his mask and the vampire gnarled toward Anthony before he placed his knife to the vampire's throat.

"I'm not the one to play around with, bloodsucker."

"Do tell."

"Where is this Bathory woman?"

"In the past."

"The past?" Amadeus asked. "Where in the past?"

"Where she always goes. Hungary."

"Let's move."

Amadeus and the Champions left for their ship, teleporting away. The vampire smirked as he and the other vampires who were sitting in the shadow disappeared from the Old Town.

Once the Champions were inside the Spellvector, Amadeus went to the files and read up on Hungary and Bathory's time. Upon his reading, he discovered she was dwelling in Hungary during the 16th Century. Amadeus went to the cockpit and headed toward the late 1500s.

III

<u>A DRINK?</u>

The Spellvector made its destination, hovering over Hungary in the year 1595. The air was damp and cold. Inside the ship, Amadeus set the coordinates for their teleportation, however, upon doing the checking, the same device began to beep. Amadeus looked, seeing the signal was coming from Cachtite Castle in Slovakia.

"Change of plans." Amadeus told the team. "We're heading to Cachtite Castle."

"Why?" Corbin asked. "What's happened?"

"The signal's reactivated. Eon must be there. We have to get the box."

"What about this vampire countess?" Anthony asked. "We just leave her be or something?"

"If there's any possibility, she will be alongside Eon when we confront him."

Anthony nodded. The team was prepared as the ship went over to Slovakia. Now, hovering and cloaked over Cachtite Castle. Sandra looked out from the window toward the castle. Corbin walked up to the window, seeing the castle himself.

"You think she's in there?"

"We'll find out when we get inside ourselves." Corbin said.

Once the team assembled, Amadeus asked if they were ready. As if they had any choice. Amadeus teleported them inside the castle and once they made entry, they were standing in what appeared to be a throne room. A red carpet laid on the marbled floors. The colors blended well with the interior stone colors. There was a chair sitting in the distance. Someone was there, in the shadows, due to the fact their eyes were glowing red in the darkness. Amadeus stood firm, staring at the eyes.

"Come out. We have words to discuss."

The eyes moved and were gone. The light from the outside hit the chair and it was empty. Amadeus yelled for the team to prepare themselves. Once they did, echoes of screeches came from above and around. Amadeus turned toward the door and saw Elizabeth Bathory in their sights. Dressed in a dark black dress, wearing a red coat over it. Her raven hair was long, and her lips looked as if they were drenched in blood, yet for style. Anthony looked, seeing her, pulled out his blades.

"This her?"

"It is." Amadeus said. "Don't strike. Not yet."

"So, you are the team he's spoke a lot about."

"Eon's told you about us?" Omega asked. "What has he lied about this time?"

"He told me everything. How you're responsible for this cause. Rallying people from across many lands for your selfish cause. How you seek the magic box he possesses."

"First off, my lady." Corbin said. "The box is not magic. But science."

"Corbin." Amadeus butted in. "No need to explain."

"I'm sure you wish to see him. Wouldn't you, Amadeus of Omega?"

"Where is he?"

"He's around. Minding his business. Until he desires to be seen, you'll have to contend with me."

"I'm sorry, Countess, we have no desire to spend time with you. We seek Eon and the box. Tell us where he is or you'll have to face my team head-on."

Elizabeth scoffed. Waving her hand toward the team.

"You believe they have a chance at defeating me?"

"I know they can."

Elizabeth sighed. Posturing herself as she stood firm in place facing the team.

"I haven't had to fight in quite a while. This will be a refresher for me. Afterwards, I'll take your blood and you know the rest. Don't you, Amadeus."

Anthony put on his mask and turned to Amadeus.

"When?"

"Now." Amadeus replied.

Crimson Mask rushed toward Elizabeth with slashes. She dodged the attacks, moving like a swift wind. Teleporting behind Anthony, she grabbed him, kicking him in the back of his knee and slamming him to the ground. The team was at a loss for words. More so was Amadeus.

"You're not that strong. History doesn't speak of you with these feats."

"History doesn't give all the details, Omega. Now, who's next?"

"Let's see if she can take us all at once." Sandra said.

"Good thinking." Corbin said, as his suit armored up.

They went for Elizabeth as Omega took out a plasma gun and fired upon her. She dodged the coming rounds while deflecting Jetlash's energy blasts and Ms. Titan's powerful punches. Elizabeth laughed, shaking her head as she waved her hands around herself and the air near her. She stopped deflecting and stood. They continued to attack, even Anthony got back up from the floor, taking out his two handguns and began firing. Amadeus paused his firing, seeing Elizabeth still.

"She's conjured a force field. Guys, stop!"

The team heard Amadeus' commanded and ceased. They

looked toward Omega as he pointed back to Elizabeth. It was there when they could see the ripples of the force field. Amadeus did not understand how she was capable of creating such defenses.

"What's wrong?" Elizabeth asked with a grin. "Too much for you and your team?"

Anthony continued firing at the force field. He walked closer and closer, continuing the fire. Elizabeth crossed her arms and stood still with a smile on her face. Amadeus tried to talk reason to Crimson Mask, yet he was not hearing any of it. He wanted to take down Elizabeth by any means. However, she lowered the field and attacked Anthony once again. Not only him, but the rest of the team with a super speed hit-and-run blow. Leaving Amadeus to see his team down.

"Don't worry." She said. "Eon told me not to harm you. Never said anything about your little team."

Amadeus sighed, raising up his gun.

"Where is Eon?"

"You'll see him soon enough. For right now, I must leave you. I have other business ventures to take care of."

Elizabeth vanished in a mist of smoke. Afterwards, Omega went and checked on his team. They were still alive, just unconscious. Amadeus shook his head in disappointment.

"I should've known."

"You can't know everything, Amadeus." A voice said from the entrance.

Amadeus stood up and saw where the voice came from. Walking out of the shadows to the door was Eon himself, holding the Cosmicbox in his hands. Amadeus quickly raised his gun.

"Hand it over, Eon."

"Is this any way to greet an old friend?"

"You're no friend of mine. Not anymore."

Eon nodded. He walked over toward the nearby table, sitting the box down. He walked away from the box even though

Amadeus' eyes were locked tight upon it.

"Look this way, Amadeus."

Amadeus moved his eyes from Eon to the box and back again. Eon grinned heavily.

"We should talk." Eon said. "Before things turn out for the worst, eh?"

"Hand over the box."

"Why should I, Amadeus? What good will it do for you?"

"More than you can understand."

"Is that a fact?"

"You know the power the box holds. The good it can do in rightful hands."

"And your hands are rightful?"

Amadeus cocked his head, keeping his eyes on Eon and the box. The team was slowly regaining consciousness as they moved around the floor, raising themselves up to see Eon and Omega staring down. Corbin rose up and quickly stood up seeing Eon.

"He's here!" Corbin yelled.

"I know." Omega replied. " I am aware."

"Your little team can't best me. Even without the box, I can decimate you all in one quick move."

The team stood to their feet, standing behind Omega. They all were injured. However, they were prepared to face Eon alongside Omega by any means. Amadeus knew this as he began to think to himself of what's next. He thought and nodded to the suggestion of his mind. His right hand reached into his coat pocket, he had something.

"You're really going to try and best me?" Eon said.

"I have something else in mind." Amadeus replied.

Omega pulled out the object in his pocket and tossed it to the ground in front of Eon. Once it made impact, the object exploded into a bright light. Eon was caught off guard as he dropped the box. Amadeus however was not affected due to his goggles as he ran over and snatched the box. He ran back to the team in haste.

"It's time to go!"

Amadeus teleported himself and the team back to the ship. Once the brightness decreased, Eon realized they were gone and so was the box.

"Clever." Eon said.

In the Spellvector, the team was prepared as Amadeus left the time-period. Returning to the Time Dimension. Afterwards, Amadeus placed the box in his lab as the team gazed toward it.

"Finally got the box." Corbin said.

"This is only the beginning." Omega replied. "We better be ready for what's next."

YONDERERS: DAYS OF OUR FUTURE

I

NUBREED FUTURE

In the city of Chicago, Illinois. At the Yonderers Mansion, Professor Edge is speaking with the younger nubreeds about possibly joining the Yonderers in the future. As he speaks to them, Lois Frost walks in.

"What is it, Frost?" Professor Edge asked.

"You need to come see this." Frost replied.

Frost and Edge left the room, heading down the hall. Edge has a worried look on his face as he has no idea what's going on. They turn left and go into the living room. Inside the living room are the Yonderers themselves, Valinor, Emerald, Crystalax, Gale, Magic Carpet, and The Surf. Edge was surprised to see John Terror and Jade Horror in the room.

"I see you both received the call."

"Figured it was of something important." Terror said.

"Agreed." Jade said.

They are all watching the television in the room as Edge watched on as well.

On the TV is the Chicago News, where the reporter is

standing in the middle of downtown Chicago as civilians run wild as the Fellowship of Nubreeds, which are Cosmic Card, Mistress Destroyer, Omega Thunder, Kudo Fox, and Jackhammer are attacking the city for reasons involving straight-edge. The reporter turns to her right and General Rilla is behind her. Rilla, who is wearing his orange and black attire, grabs the reporter's microphone and looked into the camera.

"Out of my way, human. Cullen Edge, you know what this scenery means. I've tried to tell you years before, this world belongs to the nubreeds now. Humans shall be extinct and don't try sending your insignificant group of pawns to stop us."

Frost turned off the TV as the room is quiet with everyone looking to Edge for answers.

"We should go after him." Terror told Edge.

"John, don't fall into his plans. It's not the way it's looking on that screen" Edge replied.

"What shall we do?" Jade Horror says to Edge.

Edge looked at the team and turned to Frost.

"Very well. Prepare for mission." Edge told Frost.

The members of the Yonderers begin walking out of the living room and heading towards the chamber. Terror looks on as everyone else leaves and Edge notices it and walks over to Terror.

"What now, John?" Edge asked Terror.

"Nothing. Though, it is about time for Rilla to be taken down.' Terror replies as he walked away.

Edge smiled as Terror walked away.

Meanwhile, in Downtown Chicago, General Rilla and his Fellowship of Nubreeds are terrorizing the city and destroying many buildings and city monuments. Rilla looked to his left and sees a famous hotel building and Tower. Rilla turns to Jackhammer with an intension in his eyes.

"Hammer! Take down this waste of bricks! Show them your power!

Jackhammer raises his huge arms up and slams them into the ground, creating a wave that is moving straight and slams into the building, crashing it down. Rilla smiles as he watches the building fall to the ground.

"This is what the humans deserve! The nubreeds are the true force of this planet. We are the future power structure." Rilla spoke.

"They don't deserve it this way." Someone said behind Rilla.

Rilla turned, seeing the Yonderers approaching him. Behind Rilla arrived the Fellowship of Nubreeds. Rilla looked on at the Yonderers, realizing Edge was not with them.

"It seems that Cullen is too afraid to fight for what's right." Rilla said.

"Doesn't matter, Raymus. What matters is that I'm going take that helmet of yours and shove it up your ass." Terror said.

Rilla, enraged as his eyes glow a violet color. He slowly raised his arms and began levitating off the road. He glared at Terror and the Yonderers before looking at the Fellowship.

"FELLOWSHIP! DESTROY THE PESTS!"

The Fellowship run towards the Yonderers as they do the same. While the two teams run toward each other, Terror stops Frost from heading directly toward Rilla.

"What are you doing, John?!" Frost asked Terror.

"You take the Fellowship. I'll take Rilla."

Frost goes ahead and runs toward the Fellowship and they collide. Cosmic Card is throwing cosmic beams at Emerald, Mistress Destroyer is fighting and swiping against Jade Horror and Lois Frost, Kudo Fox is shooting his pistols at Valinor as he blocks them with a electric force field and yelling out sarcastic remarks, Gale and Magic Carpet are fighting off Omega Thunder as he shoots lightning bolts, and Crystalax. The Surf held back

Jackhammer from doing more damage. Rilla sits and watches the battle and looks to his left, seeing Terror.

Terror takes off his black leather trench coat and places on his metallic claw gloves. Rilla sees him and moves closer to Terror with his arms crossed.

"How foolish for a man with metal bones to face me." Rilla said to Terror.

"Let's go, diffy."

Rilla begins firing blasts of purple electric beams toward Terror. He dodges them and lunges over to Rilla, but slams into a electric force field created by Rilla. Rilla uses his magnetic ability to pick up Terror and begins slamming him into a wall of a nearby building and onto the ground.

"They don't call me the *Lord of Magnecution* for nothing." Rilla said as he continues slamming Terror into the wall and onto the ground.

While Rilla and Terror battled, the Yonderers are losing against the Fellowship. Cosmic Card has defeated Emerald with his cosmic maneuvers, Frost and Horror defeated Mistress Destroyer by a combination of attacks. Frost looks over at Jade with an envious look. Jade looked over to Frost, seeing her facial expression.

"Is there a problem?"

"No. You're just the problem." Frost replied.

"Envious and jealous."

Kudo Fox dodged Valinor's flying cards and shoots Valinor in the leg and he falls to the ground, struggling to stand up and he looks up and Fox runs over to him and kicks him in the head, knocking him out.

"That's how you defeat someone." Fox says while smiling.

Omega Thunder defeated both Gale and Magic Carpet by blasting a lightning ball at Carpet and slamming Gale into the ground with a thunder-tackle. Jackhammer defeated Surf, while continuing to slam Crystalax into the ground and picks him up and throws him into a nearby wall, smashing him through the wall. Rilla has defeated Terror by exhausting him, though he spots Horror and Frost running toward him.

"I'll finish this myself."

Rilla conjures up a magnetic force field, which pulls Horror onto the force field, electrocuting her due to her metallic skeleton. Frost tries to knock down the force field by shooting ice beams at the field, but it has no effect. Rilla laughs as Frost continues to try knocking it down.

"You can stop now, Ms. Frost." Rilla said. "You'll tired yourself out before you make a dent into this field."

Frost looks at Rilla and she is slammed by an electric beam from Rilla. Frost is defeated as well as Jade. Rilla looks around and sees that he and his Fellowship have won. Rilla and the Fellowship celebrate, but Rilla wants to do more damage to the city, and he blasts the Willis Tower and it begins falling apart and Rilla, along with the Fellowship flee the area. After the tower collapses, police officers and SWAT trucks arrive at the scene and only see the defeated Yonderers, laid out on the ground. Terror gets to his knees and sees himself surrounded by a circle of SWAT members, pointing their guns at him.

"This is nice." Terror said.

Later, the Fellowship arrive at their warehouse hideout along with Rilla. Omega Thunder asked Rilla what they should do now and Rilla turns and looks.

"Fellowship. We have already dealt with those Yonderers. Now, we have a bigger task in front of us. That task is called Glasco, Incorporated. Its CEO, Ezekiel McKnight is currently working with the Professor Mite on building these huge sentinel machines. These machines are built for sole purpose of accomplishing one goal: Exterminate nubreeds from the face of this earth."

"Why would they build such a thing to destroy us?" Fox asked. "What have we truly done to them to receive negative attention?"

"They don't want our kind to exist because we pose a threat toward the humans. Now, we must do the only thing to stop such a cause. We must assassinate both McKnight and Mite before their planning is finished."

During the evening, the Yonderers were able to return home from the Chicago jail and Edge walks into the main room and sees them tired and distraught from the downtown battle.

"Do any of you realize the damage you've caused in the city! Do you understand that this will bring more trouble for our kind and increase the production of enemies more so."

Terror, holding his left arm and with his trench coat hanging over his right shoulder, looks over at Edge.

"Professor. We've been through enough today."

"What do you think I was going to say? Good job? Excellent work? No! You've destroyed most of downtown! Now you guys are going to pay for the damages yourselves have created."

"Fair enough." Terror says as he walks upstairs.

The rest of the team heads to their rooms and Frost walks over to Edge as Jade looks on.

"Professor. Everything will be ok." Frost said.

"Yes, it will. That's why I'm going on a vacation and Papa Afterlife is taking my place."

"WHAT?! A vacation?! And Afterlife?!"

"Yes, I'm going on a vacation to an undisclosed location, while you and the rest of the team follow Afterlife's leadership. Now, good night, Lois."

Edge leaves for his room as Frost stands there will a shocked look on her face. Frost turns to head to her room and sees Jade standing on the stairs.

"Something wrong?" Jade asked.

"No. Nothing's wrong."

Frost walked past Jade, heading down the hall.

Jade continued upstairs to her room. Walking through the hallway, she passed by Terror's room. Seeing him healing his injuries.

"You still appear to be injured?"

"I'll be fine. It'll heal soon enough. You already know that"

"Do you need a massage or something to relax your muscles?" Jade asked.

He looks over at Jade and allows her to give him a massage on his shoulders. As she gives him the massage. Jade gave a look toward the door, Terror noticed it.

"Who's at the door, Jade?"

"No one."

During the time of midnight, a secret meeting is being held at the T.I.T.A.N. between Colonel Evan Nader and Nathan Hawke, CEO of Hawke Enterprises. They speak about the upcoming sentinel machines that will be presented tomorrow morning in Washington D.C. They sit in one of the office rooms talking amongst themselves.

"What do you think of these machines, Hawke?"

"I believe the machines will prove to be great in function, but as for military warfare, they will not be so great."

"These machines aren't being used for the military for war reasons."

"Then what are they being used for?" Hawke asked.

"They're being used to exterminate the nubreed race. Wipe

them out permanently without human casualties.”

Hawke stood up, looking at Nader. Nader stands up as well.

“Nader, I don’t agree with the fact that these machines are being used as extermination tools.”

“It’s what its made for.”

“What I’m thinking about is why you and T.I.T.A.N. are agreeing with them in the first place?” Hawke said.

“We’re not. We disagree with Glasco and the government about this project. This isn’t what T.I.T.A.N. was created for. We look to protect everyone, not exterminate them.”

“Ok, see, I’m still ongoing enough trouble with the government over the Nano Man suits.”

“Thought you had that settled.”

“You would think. After the whole *Octagon Incident*, they’ve gotten stronger with demands. Making threats. You know, their nature.”

“I’m aware of that, Hawke. I saw your press conference on CNN last week.“

“Did you enjoy it?” Hawke says with enthusiasm.

“It was funny. I’ll give you that. President Trump’s face was hilarious.”

“He’s familiar with my talk.”

Nader and Hawke shake hands and Hawke leaves the facility as Nader walks over to a computer desk, which monitors areas that other heroes and enemies reside. On the monitors were recording footage of the Yonderer Mansion, Hawke Manor, Cherub Enterprises, and even the Citadel of Enchantment.

“We have to keep eyes on everything.” Nader said.

The next day at the Yonderer Mansion, everyone is in the living room as they watch the announcement of the machines on CNN. At the event, the presenter announces Ezekiel McKnight and Professor Arthur Mite. They both walk onto the stage and Ezekiel holds the microphone as thousands of civilians stand in front of them and millions watching around the world.

"Here comes more trouble for us." Terror said.

As they watch the news, Professor Edge, dressed in a white suit, approached the team, saying goodbye as he left. As the door closed in comes Papa Afterlife, who will lead the team until Edge's unknown return.

"Look who's here." Frost said, seeing Afterlife.

"Is there a problem, Lois?" Afterlife said.

"No problem. Just announcing your arrival to the team."

"Very well."

Afterlife proceeded down the hall.

In Washington D.C., McKnight and Mite stood in front of a podium amongst a crowd of witnesses.

"Me and Professor Arthur Mite are here to present to you all the newest tech that will aid us in our battles in this life against foes foreign and domestic."

"These machines will be superior to any form of military tech. Much stronger than a tank and much faster than your little planes." Professor Mite said.

"This tech was designed and will be used for one purpose only."

Watching the news, Valinor watched on as were the others.

"Wonder what the reason is?" Valinor asked.

"Probably to keep them from going bankrupt." Terror replied. "Most organizations operate in these matters."

"These machines are the sole purpose of eradicating all of the nubreeds in the earth. Every one of them." McKnight said.

Everyone in the living room jumped from McKnight's words. All except for Terror and Jade.

"That's not right!" Surf yelled, pointing at the television.

"Great." Valinor gestured. "We're now enemies of the US Government."

"It was coming sooner or later." Terror said.

"But, why would they do such a thing?" Frost questioned.

"You guys don't see what's really going on do you."

McKnight continued to speak on how the machines will eliminate the nubreed population to make Earth a save place for humanity. Nathan Hawke sat in the audience as did Evan Nader.

"That's utter bullshit right there." Terror said.

McKnight handed the microphone to Professor Mite, who took the stage. Looking out at the audience.

"Ladies and gentlemen, we present to you, the new force upon the world, the Nubreed eradicators, Here they are… the *STEELERS!!!*"

The curtains behind Mite and McKnight open up, revealing four colossal sentinel machines that stand approximately twenty to forty feet tall and weighing between ten and twenty tons. The eyes of the Steelers lit up and they begin to walk and strike a pose to get the audience to cheer for them. The Steeler in the center scanned the audience for any signs of a nubreed and Nathan looked around, hoping that there weren't any nubreeds in the audience. The Steeler stood up and straight. McKnight and Mite followed suit.

Coming in front of them is Rilla and his Fellowship. The audience looked on as they saw Rilla and the Fellowship approaching the stage. Nathan and Nader try to evacuate the audience, but no one will leave the area, as they know that something bad is about to happen.

Rilla reached the stage, staring at McKnight and Mite. The Fellowship stood behind him. Rilla turned to his right, gazing up at the Steelers and looking back to McKnight and Mite.

"This is what you think is best for the world, Homo-Sapiens?!"

"The world needs these beings to rid itself of scum like you and the rest of your poisoned kind." McKnight said.

"Besides, it's your fault. Especially with the cause of the downtown Chicago battle between your guys and those young children." Mite added.

Rilla gave a look toward his Fellowship and raised his arm, pointing at McKnight.

"Kudo! Show them your sharp shooting."

"With pleasure, General." Kudo replied with a smile.

Kudo took out his pistols, aiming toward McKnight. Before taking the shot, he's kicked by the center Steeler and now the other three Steelers are activated and Rilla saw it without haste, commanding his Fellowship to combat the four Steelers, while he goes to handle McKnight and Mite. The Fellowship attacked the Steelers with all their might, but what they noticed was how the Steelers had all their abilities and techniques. The Steelers began firing beams from their palms toward the Fellowship. The audience now in panic mode, running amok all-over downtown Washington D.C. Nathan and Nader continued to get people to leave the area.

"Oh, now they get the sense to leave." Hawke says.

The Steelers are now defeating the Fellowship while Rilla attacked McKnight by slamming him into a wall and throwing Mite into the scattered audience. He turned around, witnessing his entire Fellowship being defeated, including the powerful Jackhammer. Rilla looked up, finding himself standing in front of the four Steelers. Rilla charged up his magnetic-electric abilities and stares as the four Steelers form a circle around him. His hands glowing as do his eyes.

"ELIMINATE TARGET." A Steeler spoke.

"If this is the way it's going to be. So be it."

Rilla attacked the Steeler standing in front of him with an electric blast, Firing the Steeler behind him into the area of the audience. Rilla shielded himself from the beam coming from the Steeler to his left and fire toward it. As he turned, the Steeler on his right deflected the electric blasts, slamming its fist into Rilla, shoving him into the ground. The Steeler picked up the General and threw him across the area, smashing him into the buildings. Nader is still in the area, although, Hawke had left.

Nader contacted T.I.T.A.N. agents to arrive and stop the four Steelers, as of now, they are not only defeating General Rilla and his Fellowship, they are also attacking civilians and setting sight on destroying the city. Mite rose to his feet as his Agency X arrived at the scene, taking him to a safer location. Glasco agents fled the area. There's nothing they can do to stop the Steelers.

The Yonderers watched on. Terror looked on and turned to the members.

"Think we should go to D.C.?" Terror asked sarcastically.

"We might have to." Frost replied.

"What are you guys preparing?" Afterlife asks as he enters the living room.

"We are preparing to head to D.C. to stop the Steelers' havoc." Terror told Afterlife.

Papa Afterlife took a small look at the team and grinned.

"You've just seen what those things can do. What makes you think that you can defeat them?"

"Because we're nubreeds." Terror said.

"You didn't seem to care when we were downtown." Frost said.

Terror gave Frost a stare. Frost smirked at him, turning to Jade, who's shaking her head. Afterlife took another look at the team.

"Well then. Prepare yourselves for the mission. I am coming along as well." Afterlife said. "See how good you people work as a unit."

"This is intriguing." Frost said.

Jade approached Frost, smiling.

"Take it from me, Afterlife doesn't play well when it comes to business. Deal with it."

The team gets prepared in their gear. Walking into the hangar, approaching the Yonder-Jet with Gale in the cockpit. Surf showed a worried look on his face, turning to Valinor.

"Is she able to fly this thing?" Surf asked.

"She's flown it before. Nothing to worry about."

Surf sighted with relief. "That's good to hear."

"Except for the landings."

"What about the landings?!" Surf shockingly asked.

Gale spoke to the team, preparing them for takeoff. The jet started to move. Surf sat tightly in his seat as the jet increased in speed.

"Here we go." Surf said to himself. "Here we go."

Now the jet is in the air heading toward Washington D.C. Emerald looked over to his right, seeing Terror wearing his black sunglasses inside of the jet.

"Why are you wearing sunglasses in the jet?"

Terror turned toward Emerald and stared for a second. Emerald shook his head, waiting for an answer. Terror didn't bulge. His body did not move nor did his focus shift.

"Because I can't see you." Terror said.

"Oh," Emerald said. "I see. You got jokes."

'How long is this flight, Gale?" Terror asked.

"Approximately an hour and forty-seven minutes, John."

"Great." Terror replied, sitting back in his seat.

Still ongoing in D.C., Nader's T.I.T.A.N. agents fight against the Steelers. The tall automatons are taking out every T.I.T.A.N. agent in their sights. Nader turned, spotting one of the Steelers staring at him. Its focus was clear. The Steeler charged up its beam and fired it toward Nader.

"Shit!"

Nader jumped out of the impact area of the blast. The blast itself, knocked Nader over to the ground. Nader took the small moment to catch his breath.

"Someone, anyone. Come help us." Nader said, watching the Steelers destroy what is in front of them.

II

THE FIGHT FOR OUR FUTURE

The T.I.T.A.N. agents continue battling the destructive Steelers in downtown D.C. Nader fired a shot toward one of the Steelers. Shooting the Steeler in its face, to which the automaton glanced down at Nader. It rose up its foot, Nader gave the entity a stare. Its foot came down as Nader jumped out of the way, hiding himself behind a beaten-down bus. Nader took out a cell phone and dialed a number. Waiting for an answer.

"Hawke." Nader said.

"Nader."

"Hawke, where the hell are you?!"

"I'm at my workplace, preparing something."

"Such as?" Nader wondered.

"I think you guys need some extra help." Hawke gestured. "Some nano-tech perhaps."

"Fair game. I'll be waiting on you." Nader answered, hanging up the call as he continued shooting toward the Steelers.

The Steelers destroy many buildings in their paths and continue annihilating the T.I.T.A.N. agents which surround them. Nader ran to a different site around the debris filled streets to hide from the Steelers. Shooting them at close range.

Meanwhile at Hawke Enterprises, Nathan went through the

Nano-Bunker, searching through his collection of Nano Man exosuits. Searching around until he spotted one and smiled.

"Time for my baby to go to work."

On the Yonder-Jet, the team prepared for the battle ahead against the Steelers. Terror, still wearing his sunglasses, took a look around at the team. Those on his side of the jet and those behind him. He looked to his side, seeing Jade and Lois sitting on opposite sides and opposite angles. Terror showed a faint smirk, shaking his head as he turned his attention to the front, looking at Gale as she piloted the jet.

"How much time is left before we hit D.C.?"

"Fifty-two minutes, John." Gale replied.

"Fifty-two minutes. Sounds great."

The others give Terror a stare. Terror saw them and their gazes. In minor retaliation, he gave them a glare. Each of them.

"What?" Terror asked.

The team turn their sights from Terror. He grinned. Valinor looked on as he listened to music on his IPhone and The Surf was playing some mobile game on his Android. The other members just talked in conversations.

"How do you feel?" Valinor asked Surf.

"Fine. Ok"

"You're still afraid, aren't you?"

"No." Surf replied, shaking his head. "Just… listen to your rock music, dude."

Valinor laughed as Surf turned up the volume on his phone.

Back in D.C. at a distant warehouse, McKnight and Mite are attempting to find way out of the city so that they won't get caught by T.I.T.A.N. or Rilla.

"Where should we go?!" Mite wondered.

"No idea. But I believe that we should leave the city before anyone catches us.”

“I agree with you, but Evan Nader knows how to track us as well as his partner, Hawke. Speaking of which, where did he go when the Steelers went amok?”

“I really don’t know. Probably just ran off to the nearest bar, if possible.”

The Steelers move through D.C. Nader is still awaiting Hawke’s back-up plan. Other T.I.T.A.N. agents ran over to Nader.

“Sir, we’re outnumbered!”

“Don’t worry, backup is coming.”

“What about the Elite Five? Where are they?”

“The Elite Five are searching for McKnight and Mite right now. They contacted me earlier.”

They continued fighting the Steelers. Rilla recovered from the previous attack and so have his Fellowship. As a means of reinforcements, other members of the Fellowship arrived. They are known as X-Manta, Eerie, The Marine, and Hunter Vazquez.

“I was wondering where you four were.” Rilla said.

“We were handling business of our own.” Vazquez replied.

“I see. Fellowship, prepare to fight the Steelers one more time and this time don’t hold back.”

The Yonderers finally arrived in D.C. Taking witness to the city’s overrun by the Steelers. The team exit the jet, staring out across the area, watching the Steelers cause major damage and destruction. Terror looked on, pulling out his glocks, checking them for ammo. Gale turned toward him as did the rest of the group.

“Best to double-check.” Terror said.

“Are you sure you’re ready for this, John?” Papa Afterlife asked.

"Ready? Afterlife, I've been ready. True question is are you ready."

Terror walked from Afterlife's sight as Jade approached him. Watching Terror move on.

"Don't worry. He's just a smartass."

"I am aware of his speech patterns, my lady."

The Yonderers head toward the area of the Steelers. While they are coming, Nader and the agents continue to shelter themselves from the Steelers' attacks. A whirring sound came from above. Nader walked out from the hiding place quieting, looking up to see The Nano Man hovering above him.

"It's about time." Nader said.

"They don't call me *The Insuperable Nano Man* for nothing."

Nano Man flew toward the Steelers. Shooting his blue energy beams, even tackled one to the ground. Nano Man stared at the Steeler on the ground and fired six missiles. The missiles impact the Steeler's shielded body, but the automaton is still active.

"What can stop these colossal machines?" Nano Man wondered.

Nano Man took a glance around the area as the Steeler arose to its feet. In doing so, smashed Nano Man to the ground with its fist. The Steeler charged up its inner parts and fired missiles back at Nano Man. The missiles collide with Nano Man's armor and some even make dents into the exosuits.

"Wow. That actually hurt." Nano Man said to himself.

Nano Man turned to his right, seeing Rilla and his Fellowship arrive. Nano Man stood up as Rilla approached him. Both were with caution. However, Rilla's stance was more focused on force than stealth

"Great. The "hardline" are here." Nano Man gestured.

"We are here to stop those nubreed hunting abominations that were created by these weak-minded fools." Rilla replied.

"At least you're here to help and not to destroy."

"Don't worry. We intend to assist as of now. But we'll destroy everything later."

Rilla sent out the command toward his Fellowship to attack the Steelers. Cosmic Card, X-Manta, and The Marine attack one of the Steelers as Mistress Destroyer and Omega Thunder collided with another one. Jackhammer and Kudo Fox attacked the other. But, Hunter Vazquez and Eerie sat back and watched. Such an action gravitated toward Rilla, who watched them.

"Why are the two of you just standing there?!"

"We're waiting for the Yonderers to arrive." Vazquez said.

Rilla paused. He understood and nodded with a grim, turning toward Nano Man. Nano Man in such an act, saw Rilla staring at him.

"So, are we gonna help your 'fellowship' or are we gonna just sit here like those pawns of yours over there?" Nano Man asked.

"They are not pawns." Rilla replied with vigor in his voice. "They are incredible members of the hardline fellowship."

Nano Man went over toward of the Steelers and fired his energy beams once more. Rilla hovered up in the air as well and began firing electric beams toward the other Steeler. Rilla blasted the Steeler, knocking it to the ground.

"You should try that, Tech One."

Nano Man glared at Rilla, turning to the Steeler in front of him. Nano Man charged up from his chest and unleashed his ultrabeam through the Steeler. Breaking it apart into pieces of metal. One Steeler down. Only three remain.

"No, I think you should try that, "General"." Nano Man said sarcastically.

While Rilla and his Fellowship fought the three remaining Steelers along with the T.I.T.A.N. agents and Nader. The Yonderers have arrived at the scene. Terror looked up to see Nano Man flying towards another Steeler.

"Great. Tech-head is here."

"Don't worry about him, Terror. At least he's helping." Afterlife said.

"Whatever. Let's end all of this."

The Yonderers charged into the battle against the Steelers. General Rilla, still in the air, gazed down, seeing Edge's team fighting. He saw Vazquez and Eerie approaching them quietly, their sights primarily on both Terror and Jade. Without haste, Terror and Jade spot Vazquez and Eerie.

"Nice to see you again, John." Vazquez said.

"Move out of the way. I'm only here to stop the machines."

"Horror." Eerie said toward Jade.

"Why are you here? There's nothing eerily about what's happening." Jade replied

Terror and Jade ran into the battle. Terror leaped into the air, climbing on the back of one of the Steelers as Jade used her fire power to burn through the Steeler's legs.

"Hey. I'm behind you." Terror yelled toward the Steeler.

The Steeler's head turned toward Terror. He lunged at the Steeler's head and begins shooting it in the eyes and in doing so, remove his sword from his coat and slicked at its neck. While Jade melted the legs, Terror slashed the neck. He paused for a moment, taking out a pistol and shot the Steeler in the head while swipes at its neck with the sword. The head fell into the ground. Two Steelers down. Two to go.

"That's how it's done." Terror said.

"Yeah. Nice going." Jade replied.

Vazquez looked at Eerie and she gave a grin. Vazquez grinned as well and the two attacked Terror and Jade in the middle of their continued attacks. The four fought each other as the Yonderers took the battle to the remaining Steelers. Rilla gathered his Fellowship as they watched the young ones using team-tactics to eliminate the Steelers. Terror tackled Vazquez while Jade and Eerie crossed punches and kicks.

"Don't you see those things?!" Terror said. "They were made to kill us. Guys like us!"

"I am aware. However, I only came to face you. Our last encounter wasn't much of a splendid time."

"I assure you, we'll have many more times to come. Provided I don't kill you sooner."

Terror kicked Vazquez in the face and held up his pistol toward his head. Vazquez froze as the muzzle of the gun touched his forehead.

"Make a move and it's all over." Terror said.

Vazquez nodded with a grin as he backed away. He looked over, seeing Eerie and Jade still throwing blows.

"Jenelle, it's time to go."

Eerie paused her attacks as she moved alongside Vazquez and the rest of the Fellowship. Rilla hovered over them, looking out toward Terror, Jade, and the Yonderers.

"I see this situation is taken care of. Till next time. When it's only us."

Rilla and the Fellowship left the area. Nano Man caught them leaving.

"The hell are they going?"

Terror and Jade turned back toward the battle and as they did, the final Steeler fell to the ground. Its legs cut off and from the debris walked out the team. Successful in this short battle. They gathered as Nano Man landed in front of them.

"Oh my." Surf said. "You're Nano Man!"

"I am. You guys did great."

"They're still learning." Terror said.

"You could learn something from them."

Terror walked up toward Nano Man before Jade managed to push him back.

"Not today." She said.

"Be catching you later." Nano Man said, flying off.

Sometime later, Nader regrouped the T.I.T.A.N. agents and they gathered up all the materials from the fallen Steelers. No word on where McKnight and Mite had gone. Rilla and his Fellowship remained in their secret place, hoping for another bout with the Yonderers. The Yonderers themselves, continued to train and hone their skills. Terror and Jade went out to find anymore traces of Agency X.

Meanwhile, in the city of Chicago, a strange essence filled the upper air. The essence was felt by Professor Edge and Papa Afterlife as they talked outside.

"You sense it too?" Afterlife asked.

"Yes. Something foreign. Something from the stars. And it's heading here."

ENFORCEMENT ORDER 66 : MISSIONS AHEAD

I

FIRST TIME OUT

A.B. waited in the briefing room for her recruits to arrive. Entering first was Gage Hark. Walking in calmly as he gave her a nod and stood against the wall near the large screen.

"I hope they were right behind you." A.B. said.

"Don't worry, ma'am. They should be coming in anytime now."

Entering the room first was *Lance Gasper*: The self-profound star of celebrity worship. He entered the briefing room as he enters any building, hoping all eyes are set on him. Second to enter was *Black Mare*, a woman with a fierce countenance and one who's solely focused on the mission at hand. Third was Daniel Barns, also known as *G-Zero*: The racer who uses speed to achieve his goals. Fourth was Randy Keith, called by most *Thunderstorm*. A being of massive bolts within him. His temper can prove the direness of matters. Fifth was Maria Swan: The wildcard of the group. A savvy young woman whose main desire is to meet Death herself. Sixth and last to enter was Blake Smalls, known by his codename: *Gunbaine*. Strangely enough to the group, Gunbaine seemed to appear a little weary.

"What's going on with you, Smalls?" Hark asked.

"Had a little run-in with The Swordman. Was hired to do a small job in protecting a crime lord. Things turned sideways. Plus, I was involved in a contest with other mercs. Didn't turn out how I hoped. Now, I'm here."

"That's all that matters." A.B. said. "Now, I am sure everyone is ready to hear you're first mission."

"I am." Gunbaine said. "What is it?"

A.B. approached the screen and upon it appeared Rabat, Morocco. The scenery of the city intrigued to group. Black Mare stepped foot closer, Maria's eyes widen, Lance removed his shades to see the screen in full. Thunderstorm, G-Zero, and Gunbaine were focused. Hark watched, monitoring the group closely.

"I'll be sending you all to Morocco. We have received Intel that Death and those who work under her have been preparing to strike the Parliament and cause the city of Rabat to delve into chaos. You will be sent there to make sure that doesn't happen."

"Wait." G-Zero said. "Hold on. You're sending us to protect the government authorities in a foreign country?"

"It's the only way we track down Death's workings. We stop one, we'll be closer to the next."

"I still don't get it."

"You don't have to." A.B. declared. "You just have to obey."

"And what if I don't?"

Hark stepped forward with his Colt M4 in hand. A.B. watched him, looked closely toward G-Zero's facial expressions. G-Zero was still as he set his eyes on Hark's M4. He nodded with respect.

"I see you have a fine weapon there, Lieutenant."

"Don't make me use it on you."

"Noted."

Hark returned to his position as A.B. continued giving the briefing. Afterwards, the team was told to gather their gear and head to the cargo plane which was prepared to take them to Rabat. Everyone grabbed what they needed. From Gunbaine's rifle and pistols to G-Zero's vehicle. Walking outside toward the plane and the team entered with an additional dozen Black Ops soldiers. Hark also entered the plane.

"A.B. has given me orders of teaming with you all on this mission. I am sure you'll do as you're told."

"We'll see." Gunbaine said.

"What's that, Smalls?"

"You heard me. No hard feelings."

"None." Hark said. "None yet."

The plane took off from Base 33. Preparing for its arrival in Rabat.

II

WELCOME TO MOROCCO

Within the plane on one side sat Gunbaine, Thunderstorm, Black Mare, and Maria Swan. On the other side was Hark, G-Zero, and Gasper with the Black Ops soldiers scattered around. Hark kept his eyes on Gunbaine and he leaned in toward him.

"I'm sure you know what to do once we make landfall."

"And what am I supposed to do?"

"You know. Trust me."

"What if I don't?"

"Then, we brought the wrong guy. Could've chose the other one."

"Between us, he wouldn't have come aboard anyhow. He's personal to the highest extent."

"I'm aware."

"So why the fuck are you talking to me about this?"

"Because you'll be leading the team on the ground. Just checking to see if your mind is as stable as A.B. would like to believe."

Gunbaine smirked. Sitting back in his seat. Maria looked over toward him and her eyes gazed at Hark.

"So, will Death be in Rabat?"

"No." Hark said. "She's in Pegasus Prison."

"But, I was told if I joined this little group that I would meet her."

"You will eventually. Right now, your task is to stop her workings. She has something set up in Rabat that endangers all who live therein. Keep the mission in the forefront of your mind. Don't fall off."

"I won't." Randy said.

Hark nodded. "That's good to hear."

After several hours, the unit arrived in Rabat at one of their military bases. Granted entry due to the connections of A.B.'s organization and authority. While they exit the plane, Hark stepped in front of them. Giving them the orders as needed. They were each split into two separate units. Six Black Ops soldiers paired to a unit. Gunbaine was paired with Maria Swan, Gasper and Hark. Thunderstorm was paired with Black Mare and G-Zero.

"Your orders stand. We received information regarding Death's plots in this city and her Reapers have been sighted roaming around certain landmarks. Now, Gunbaine's unit will be heading toward the Riad District. Thunderstorm's unit will be set in place around Rabat Hassan.

"What are we looking for?" Black Mare asked.

"You're looking for the Reapers. They were last seen placing strange objects into the ground. What for? We aren't sure. But, that why we're here. To find these objects and stop whatever Death has planned for this city. Understood."

"Clearly." G-Zero uttered. "We get the memo."

"Then let's get moving."

The units moved out toward the destinations. While making their moves, Maria spotted large crowds of tourists going about their day. She jumped with joy.

"We have an audience!"

"No." Gunbaine said. "They're not our audience. Leave them be."

"You touch any of them, I'll cap your knee." Hark said. "You got that?"

"Always taking the fun out of things."

"So, what are we supposed to do when we see a Reaper?" Lance asked.

"We take them down."

"By knocking them out or killing them?"

"We need more information on Death's workings. Knock 'em out. If some resist, kill them."

"I'm sorry, but, is that what A.B. wants us to do?"

"Yes, Gunbaine. Her orders. You follow and obey."

"Right, follow and obey. Kind of like what you're doing right now."

"Don't start a fight you can't win."

"Oh, I can win it. Mere seconds of a bout is what it'll be."

"Is that right?"

"Yeah."

Maria stepped in between the two gunsmiths with a smile on her face. Patting them on their chests.

"Save you manpower for the Reapers, alright. No need to blow each other's head off."

"Lady's got a point." Gunbaine said.

"For the moment anyway."

Reaching the Riad District, Gunbaine noticed something odd with the area. Hark spotted his concerned looks.

"What's the matter with you? Got to take a shit?"

"Something's wrong. We're heading for a trap."

"Paranoid as usual."

The unit was immediately ambushed by the Reapers. Diving out from all over the District. Everyone moved to their positions with Gunbaine and Hark primarily firing at the Reapers. Tourists and civilians took off after the first shots were fired, clearing the area. It suited both sides well.

"I'll take them in the front!" Gunbaine yelled.

"I got the front!" Hark replied.

"Take another spot! I have the front!"

"Do you job!" Hark yelled back.

Gunbaine rushed to the front, firing rounds against the Reapers. Their cloaked hoods maneuvered them well enough to dodge fire. Hark moved through the area, now contacted by the opposite team. Hearing gunshots in their area. They too are also fighting the Reapers. Hark knows the battle has begun. Maria dove out from her hiding spot and attacked a Reaper standing near her, hitting him from behind with a crowbar and upper-cutting him with a high kick. Lance Gasper maneuvered and dodged the attacks before using the pavement as a source of weaponry.

The streaks of lighting were seen in the sky and the thunder followed, catching the attention of Gunbaine's unit and the Reapers around them.

"You heard that?" Hark asked.

"Yeah." Gunbaine said. "Keith's giving them hell over there."

Thunderstorm was surely giving the Reapers hell over in the Rabat Hassan area. G-Zero moved with speed, taking out the Reapers near him as Black Mare delivered serious blows to the Reapers near her with a Kevlar-laced whip. The Reapers tried shooting Keith from the sky, but, he scoffed and blasted them with lightning strikes.

Gunbaine continued firing against the Reapers and in the midst of the ongoing fight, a Reaper moved through the district, carrying a vertical object. A metallic device. The Reaper slammed the device into the concrete, causing the bottom of the device to latch into the ground. The top opened and the Reaper pressed a button.

"Gunbaine! Stop that Reaper!" Hark yelled.

Gunbaine ran for the Reaper and as he inched closer to capturing him, the round began to quake. Shocking both units.

"The hell's going on?!" Hark asked.

"Earthquake!" Gunbaine yelled!

"A big one at that!" Maria added.

The earthquake's strength increased as Gunbaine tried to pull the device out of the ground. It's too deep and latched too tight to the concrete. Hark ran up to Gunbaine.

"We have to get back to the plane now!"

Both units ran for the plane as the ground began to crack, the buildings started to shake. Windows started to burst as they came closer to the plane. As they reached the plane, Reapers were waiting for them and the remaining Black Ops soldiers took them out without hesitation. Gunbaine was impressed as they entered the plane and left Rabat.

"What's the plan now? Gunbaine asked.

"We return to Base. Find out what A.B. wants to do."

"What about the city?" G-Zero asked.

"The Moroccan Government will consult with the United Nations. They'll be fine. Say it was some underground issue. Pipes in bad shape. Some shit like that."

"You're familiar with this aren't you?" Gunbaine asked.

"Don't act like you've never done the same before."

III

ENFORCEMENT VS. EXCHANGE

The Enforcement Order returned to Base 33 and A.B. took in their responses before giving them a small moment of separation. The following day, she spoke with Hark about the next mission and as such, he regrouped the team, bringing them back into the briefing room.

"Another mission." Gunbaine said. "That was quick."

"Well, this one isn't much for shocker, Smalls." Hark replied. "Just keep your ears open."

A.B. stood by the monitor, speaking of the next mission. This mission was focused on the assassination of a government official. The set location was Bosnia. G-Zero scoffed in his seat.

"You have something to say, speedy?" Hark asked.

"Another foreign country. Why not someone here. In America.'

"Because it isn't on the radar." A.B. said.

"So, what's the full objective?" Gunbaine asked. "Just for clarity."

"You find this government official. You kill him."

Gunbaine nodded.

"Just like that?"

"Just like that." A.B. grinned. "Any problems?"

"None.' Gunbaine replied. "When do we head out?"

Hark stepped forward to the door. Gunbaine stood up from his seat and walked over. The others followed Gunbaine's movements. They walked outside to the plane as previous and headed out toward Bosnia.

"So, this plan is basically finding the official, kill him, and the job's done?" Gunbaine asked.

"Seems to be the case." Thunderstorm replied.

"That is the answer." Hark said. "Any concerns?"

"None."

"What about any of you?"

"I'm peachy." Maria said.

"I'm cool with it." Lance said.

"As long as we get this done quick, I'm fine." G-Zero said.

Hark nodded with a stern look. He was ready for anything.

Upon arriving in Bosnia, After the team left the plane and headed out toward the precise location of where the official resided, they saw another team in the distance. They learned of something peculiar. Something which was not expected of a group like theirs. Neither Hark or A.B. could've foreseen what was standing in the grounds of Bosnia. However, this team was not seeking to eliminate the government official, they were protecting him.

"A.B." Hark said on his speaker. "We have a problem."

"What problem?"

"Another unit is here."

"What other unit?"

"The Exchange Force."

The Enforcement looked out, seeing the five members of the Exchange Force. Armored from head to toe and geared with weaponry beyond their requirements. Gunbaine looked over toward Hark. Hark had no words. Only concerns.

"How are we going to get through them?"

"You tell me." Hark replied. "I got nothing."

Gunbaine nodded. He looked at his teammates.

"I'll take the first shot."

"Gunbaine don't" Hark said. "If you do, they'll kill us."

"Either we die, or they die. Choice is simple."

"I'm with Gunbaine." Thunderstorm said with a nod.

Gunbaine nodded back and focused his sniper rifle toward one member of the Force. The lean one.

"Here we go."

Gunbaine fired the round and it impacted the armored Force member, knocking him to the ground. The other four looked out for anything as the lean member rose to his feet. They scoped out the area and one of them saw the rifle in the distance.

"There."

Gunbaine realized they found their spot. He looked at Hark. No emotion as the Exchange Force was heading their direction. The team was ready for the fight, standing out in the open road facing them.

"We need a new strategy."

THE IRE OF FLASHBURN: I AM SHADEBURN

I

<u>FLAMED DARKNESS</u>

Floyd Rizzo was renowned with his newfound power. A gift from the Incandescence. After Floyd's battle with the man who called himself the Atomic Bomb, Floyd understood the powers he possessed must be taken with caution and certainty. Now, after some time, he has fully begun to embrace his role as Flashburn, the vessel for the Incandescence.

Floyd practiced his combustion of flames. The presence it brought before him and how he could maneuver it. Elsewhere, Professor Dan Simon continued his research in studying the history of the Incandescence and its power's effects upon Floyd. How the power could sharpen his mind, body, and will. A knock came from the Professor's door and he looked up from his desk, seeing a woman.

"Ma'am." he said. "Need something?"

"Are you Professor Dan Simon?"

"I am. Who's asking?"

"I am. Jessica Jacobs. P.I."

"Oh." Simon nodded. "And why is a private investigator

visiting me in my working hours?"

"I've come to ask you about the incident that happened in town. About the Flashburn."

"And why would I know anything of him?"

"You were seen at the site after he defeated the Atomic Bomb guy."

"I was."

"Then, you don't mind answering my questions."

"I don't. but, can we do this tomorrow. I have work that must be done. For my student's sake."

Jessica nodded.

"Very well. I'll return tomorrow and you'll tell me all I need to know."

"I will."

Jessica left the lab as Simon was now concerned about this investigator's sudden visit. However, as Simon is in his work, he returned to it and after several minutes, Jessica's arrival was an afterthought.

Elsewhere, at a community event placed in a park in which was centered around nature and many who were at the event were certainly naturalists, activists, and ecologists. The total amount of people at this event added up to four-hundred and fifty. All were focused on the preservation of earth's natural state. They spoke highly of combating climate change and fixing the environment. Most of their ideas would conflict with the current laws of society. However, they were determined to make things right.

As the leading spokesperson talked, a figure emerged from the large tree nearby. It had the figure of a human and no face could be seen. The figure stood amid the people. For it was nightfall and the figure blended in like a dark cloak. The only light source around them was the moon's glint and candlelight.

"We will make things right." The Spokesperson said. "We are the only ones who can achieve this!"

The figure grunted and extended its arms with force, causing all the people to be swallowed up in deep darkness. Others who saw this from a distance ran in fear. The spokesperson was standing still. Frozen as the darkness consumed them. As a man ran from the scene, he looked back and saw the figure. The darkness was emitting from its hands and it appeared to glow and spark like a fire. The man ran as the figure vanished into the darkness itself.

II

SHADOWS OF THE MYSTERY

The news broke out concerning the massacre of the community event. The following day, Professor Simon and Floyd listened to news reports of what took place. On one broadcast, a reporter spoke with the man who saw the figure.

"And you said you saw who was responsible?"

"I did."

"And who was it? What did they look like?"

"They looked like darkness. Pure darkness, but with a hint of a flame. It looked similar to that Flashburn guy, but darker."

"You heard that" Simon asked.

"I did."

Simon looked at the clock and remembered. Floyd saw him moving over to his desk, placing files atop.

"What's going on, Professor?"

"There was a woman who came by yesterday. She wants to know about you. Your alter-ego."

"Did you tell her?"

"No. but, she's on her way to question me. It was a scheduled arrangement."

"I understand." Floyd said. "I'll head out there. See what I can find."

"Be careful out there." Simon said. "If these people believe you were responsible, you'll have a target on your head.

Floyd nodded and left the lab.

In the crowds of reporters, Jessica moved through them. Her purpose was separate from those of the media. As she moved through the crowds, she confronted the witness.

"I need to ask you some questions."

"But, I've already given my details."

"To the media." Jessica said, holding up a badge. "I'm not the media."

"You're a private investigator."

"I am. What did you see? Truthfully."

"Well, whomever it was looked just like Flashburn. Except you couldn't see the outfit. The figure was covered in darkness. Like a thick shadow."

"And this darkness killed these people?"

"As if it suffocated them. I'm sure they couldn't breathe in that mass."

"Suffocated?" Jessica questioned.

"Yeah. You could hear their screams muffled by the darkness."

Jessica took in the witness' statement and let him go about his business. She looked around the park, seeing multiple reporters, cameras, and interviews taking place. As she went to turn around towards the crime scene, she saw a woman who was staring into the sky. She wore a white coat, jeans, and her orange hair glistened to the sunlight. She looked to the sky herself and only saw the sun and the clear sky. She looked back to the woman with confusion.

"I'm sorry, ma'am. But, what do you see up there?"

"The sun. it's beautiful isn't it? The clear, blue sky. This calls for a peaceful day."

"I'm sorry, you're standing in a park which is covered by reporters. People died here yesterday."

"I'm aware."

"So, why are you in the park?"

"Who are you, miss?"

"Jessica Jacobs. Private Investigator. And you are?"

"Natalia Spear. I'm a solar scientist. I also study radiation. To the effect of nature and humans."

"A scientist. That's fair. However, this crime was not committed by sunlight or radiation. But, darkness. A shadow as witnesses claim."

"They say a lot when in fear. I say otherwise."

"What do you say?"

"Flashburn. I believe he was responsible. Covered his flames in darkness and scorched the people."

"How can you be sure?"

"Because there's radiation all in the grounds where the killing took place."

"There's radiation out here?" Jessica asked with caution.

"Yes. I told the officials, but they brushed me off. I sure people will be sick after this."

Jessica looked around and everyone was going about their duties. She turned back to Natalia with great concern.

"You must tell them again. Tell them you're a scientist. That radiation is in your field."

"No." Natalia said. "Best they learn from experience."

Natalia nodded and left the park, leaving Jessica in a strait of warning the people or leaving them to their reporting. She couldn't make a choice as she looked at her watch and knew she had a meeting with Professor Simon. She did not want to be late and she left the park.

Elsewhere, Floyd was up in the sky as Flashburn, scanning the grounds for anything unusual. He couldn't trace anything, but somewhere on the ground. Someone was watching him, and their eyes were covered in darkness.

III

I AM SHADEBURN

Jessica had arrived at the laboratory and sat with Professor Simon. The lab was quiet as usual. Jessica wanted a solid silent space to get her questions across to Simon, it's her preferred way of questioning. Simon sat calmly at his desk, facing Jessica who sat in front of him.

"First off, have you ever been in contact with Flashburn?"

"In contact in what form?"

"Face-to-face. Short sightings. Unusual meet-ups?"

"I can't say that I have."

Jessica nodded, writing down Simon's answers in her notepad. Simon saw how quick she could write. Her handwriting looked sloppy from a distance but very clear to understand the closer one would get. But, she would never let anyone see inside the notepad. For her eyes only. The Professor raised himself up in the seat, sitting still.

"You must know something."

"Why do you assume I know anything about Flashburn?"

"Because you were seen at the event of the fight between him and the Atomic Bomb."

"And your source is?"

"A witness at the battle claimed to have seen you. Described you very clearly."

"Did they?"

"You don't deny it?"

"Never said I did or didn't. Although, I am interested as to who this 'witness' is. Tell me, did they give you a name?"

"That's undisclosed information, Professor."

"How?"

While they spoke, a door was shut outside of the lab and through the windows Simon could see Floyd approaching the door and as he went to stand up, Floyd entered the lab, seeing the Professor and Jessica at the desk. Jessica turned to see Floyd. Curious.

"And who are you?" She asked.

"I'm Floyd Rizzo. A student of Professor Simon."

"Ah. A student. I didn't know you had students, Professor."

"Floyd's a great student. He's learned a lot under my tutelage. I am curious as to why Floyd has come."

"I have news to give you concerning our project."

"What of the project?"

"I couldn't trace the source of the problem."

"No sign of it?" The Professor asked. "Nothing out of the ordinary?"

"Nothing."

Jessica looked at Floyd and Simon with interest, turning to face them back and forth.

"I'm curious. What's this project you're both working on?"

"I'm sorry, ma'am. The project is under undisclosed circumstances."

Jessica stared at Simon, who grinned.

"I see." Jessica closed her notebook. "Well, I believe I have everything I need."

"Oh good." Professor said, standing up from his chair. "I bid you good luck on your case."

"Same to your project."

They shook hands and without warning, the ground trembled.

Shaking the laboratory. Floyd looked around seeing frames shaking on the walls. Simon held the computer monitor still.

"What was that?" Jessica asked.

"I'm not certain." Simon replied. "Floyd, what is it?"

"Someone's outside." Floyd said, looking into the air.

"How do you know someone's outside?" Jessica questioned. "Is he a psychic or something?"

Floyd left the laboratory, Simon and Jessica followed him. Leading to the outside parking lot, they saw a figure standing still. Cloaked in the shadows of its own body. Floyd stepped forward.

"That's the suspect." Jessica said.

"I've come to meet him." The figure spoke in an eerie wavy voice. "My counterpart of the flames. Of the fire."

"Did you cause the quake?" Floyd asked.

"To bring out my counterpart. I know he's here."

"Counterpart?" Jessica said. "What's he talking about?"

"I'm not sure." Simon replied.

"Who's your counterpart?" Floyd asked.

"The one of the Incandescence. Flashburn."

Floyd stared as Simon shook his head and Jessica looked closer at the shadow figure. Its appearance and the slight references to a uniform underneath the cloaked darkness.

"What's your name?" Floyd asked.

"I am Shadeburn."

"Floyd, it's him." Simon pointed.

Floyd took in the notion of Shadeburn's interior motives. He could feel them within himself, clawing through his chest. He could also feel the flames of the Incandescence within him, slowly kindling from within. The heat was increasing.

"I know what must be done, Professor." Floyd said confidently.

"In front of the investigator?"

"I have no choice."

Floyd stepped forward before Shadeburn. Jessica looked somewhat off at Floyd's posture and position. She turned to Simon who was solely focused on Floyd's well-being, however, there was no fear in his expression. He had great confidence in his student.

"What's he doing?"

"You're about to find out." The Professor said. "You're about to find out everything."

The figure glared toward Floyd, looking around the laboratory lot.

"Where is he? I know he's here. I can sense the fire within."

Floyd stepped closer. Only a few feet between him and Shadeburn. Simon and Jessica stood by the door of the laboratory. Shadeburn took another look at Floyd, now he realized something. Something within Floyd. A smile revealed itself on Shadeburn's face.

"Ah. You're him."

Floyd closed his eyes and upon opening them, they were covered in flames. He extended his hands and a great whirlwind of fire appeared around him, brightening the parking lot. Within the whirlwind, Floyd had transformed into Flashburn. Once the whirlwind ceased, Flashburn was revealed. Jessica saw and now she knew. Floyd is Flashburn.

"You don't belong here." Flashburn said.

"I'm right where I should be."

"Fair enough."

Flashburn bolted into the sky and Shadeburn followed. The two entities battled it out in the sky. Firing fire and shadows against one another with great force. Both were evenly matched. However, Shadeburn teleported behind Flashburn and grabbed him with a mist of darkness, blocking his eyesight. While Flashburn fought to regain his vision, Shadeburn snatched him by his right ankle and tossed him to the pavement of the parking lot.

Flashburn removed the mist from his eyes, seeing clearly once again.

"My master has commanded me to eliminate you." Shadeburn said.

"And who is your master?"

"My. You don't know? Your master hasn't told you all things. A shame. A pity for one who calls himself a mentor."

Flashburn arose and went for a strike, but Shadeburn was too quick, elwoing him in the face and causing him to crash from the blow and of his own speed. Flashburn laid on the ground as Shadeburn glanced up to the sky.

"We'll do this again very soon, Flashburn."

Shadeburn evaporated into a dark cloud and was gone. Simon ran toward Flashburn as he reverted to Floyd. Out of breath, yet there were no bruises or blood. Simon asked him if he was alright and not in any pain. Floyd replied with calmness. He was well. Jessica approached them cautiously.

"You have a lot to tell me." Jessica said.

"Only if you can handle it." Simon replied.

IV

MATTER BETWEEN DARKNESS AND FIRE

Returning inside the lab, Simon wanted to check Floyd for more possible injuries, but Floyd was well. No bruises, cuts, or marks. Still no sign of blood. Jessica watched as the two were calm and collective after what previously happened.

"You two aren't shaken up?"

"Why would we be?" Simon replied.

"Because that thing, whatever it was, looked like a walking shadow. And what it did to him."

"Don't worry about me." Floyd said. "I'll be fine."

"So, you're him. The Flashburn."

"I am. Have you been seeking me out?"

"Well, I spoke with your Professor about him yesterday and he claimed not to know anything about Flashburn. That's why I'm here today. To learn more of what he knew. But, I see that now I know a lot more than what I was expecting."

"I said what I had to in order to protect Floyd."

"I see that now." Jessica said. "After all, he's your student. I wouldn't expect a Professor to do less than that."

"What did you want to ask?" Floyd said.

"Why are you here? Where do your abilities come from?"

Floyd sat up in the chair, facing Jessica. He sighed.

"I was given these abilities. Before all of this, I was just a young engineer looking to make a living for myself. I was led to a place where I met a entity, called the Incandescence. He granted me these abilities and proclaim that I would become his vessel, the Flashburn."

"You're telling me some kind of supernatural being gave you these powers?"

"I wouldn't call him supernatural." The Professor added. "More like elemental."

Jessica scoffed. "So, where is he now?"

"I do not know. He appears when necessary."

"How come he didn't show up when you were fighting that shadow out there?"

"I handled it."

"Not as good as you think." Jessica said. "You could've been killed from the fall."

"I'm alive aren't I? I know the risks of this task."

"I'm only saying, if this elemental was as powerful as you say, wouldn't he have come in at the brink moment of time and assisted you? I mean, that shadow proved himself to be much stronger than you."

"He was." Floyd said with certainty. "And I don't know how or why?"

"Why don't you ask him. This elemental of yours."

"I'm not sure you wish to see him with your own eyes."

"Has the Professor seen him?"

"I have not." Simon replied. "Although, I believe he appears only to speak to Floyd and Floyd only."

"I don't think he has much of a choice now."

"Many have spoken of me in such a way." A voice rumbled from behind Jessica.

She turned and as Floyd and the Professor saw, the Incandescence was standing before them in the middle of the laboratory. His body was of pure fire, yet no heat could be felt in the lab and the floors were not burnt. The eyes of the

Incandescence shined of a brightly lit flame. The Professor was astonished, and Jessica was afraid.

"You're him." Jessica said.

"I am who you speak of. I did not appear to aid my apprentice in this manner. For, he handed it well and he still lives because of it."

Floyd stood up from the chair and walked toward the Incandescence.

"I need to know. Who was that shadow? Where did he come from?"

"Shadeburn. I have not heard that name in ages."

"Who is he?"

"He is the living vessel of a counterpart. The one called the Luminescence. Whereas I dwell in the fires, the Luminescence dwells in the shadows. In a place of pure darkness. Yet, sometimes even his darkness can glow like a flame. Which is what you witnessed this day."

"How can I stop him?"

"You cannot. Not yet."

"How come?" The Professor asked. "Why can't Floyd stop this Shadeburn?"

"Because the others must be awoken first in order to bring forth the elemental wages of a era."

"Elemental wages?" Jessica said. "You guys pay each other or something? Give one another gifts?"

"The wages are for the generations. The wages themselves are our power. I have already given my wages to Floyd Rizzo. Now, it seems the Luminescence has given his. It only means the others will do the same very shortly."

"Others?" Floyd asked. "You mean there's more than yourself and this Luminescence?"

"Many more." The Incandescence confirmed. "Recount the number of elements which sit upon, within, and above the earth.

Think of how much power one such as I wield and what wages must be given to those worthy of the cause."

"Earth, wind, fire, air, water, darkness." The Professor said.

"What about light?" Jessica asked. "If darkness is one of the elements, light must be one as well."

"For the balance of all things, yes. However, as I am aware, there remain eight of us."

"Well, what's the eighth element?" Floyd asked.

"The spirit."

Floyd, Simon, and Jessica took in all the Incandescence had revealed unto them and noted it well.

"I must go now." The Incandescence said. "I request you all prepare yourselves for what is to come."

"And that would be?" Jessica asked.

"A change of reality. The heroes have already risen and now, the world you live in belongs to them. For the season."

Floyd bowed before the Incandescence as he disappeared in their sights in the form of a whirlwind. Floyd turned back to the Professor and Jessica as they saw his mannerisms toward the fire entity. Floyd's behavior was strikingly different when the Incandescence stood in the room. A sense of respect and honor was known and felt within the laboratory.

"What's next?" The Professor asked.

"We get ready." Floyd said. "If I'm only one of the eight, we must search for the others."

TOR-ZAR: DINOSAURS AND WEREWOLVES

I

<u>SIGNS OF A VISITOR</u>

On a clear day across the Avago Land, a swarm of Pteranodons invaded the lands of the Wanigo Tribe. Every man, woman, and child came out of their homes to fight against the aerial forces. Using bows and arrows, spears, and slingshots against the flying creatures. From the woods, bolted out Kujo, the saber-toothed liger, who jumped up, lunging at one of the Pteranodons, snatching the bird by its neck and twisting. Behind Kujo appeared Tor-Zar and with him was Sahara.

"We've come to help." Tor-Zar told the tribe.

Tor-Zar used his own bow and arrow to eliminate the Pteranodon in his sights. While some attempted to dive down toward him, he raised his spear, decorated with metallic enhancements, and slashed the birds. Sahara did the same with a spear of her own. After killing some of the birds, the rest retreat. Clearing the sky above them tribes' land. Tor-Zar and Sahara approached the Tribes leader with a kneeling bow. The utmost respect.

"It is good of you to come and aid us."

"We live here as well." Tor-Zar said. "I must ask, what caused the Pteranodons to invade your lands?"

"We found some peculiar footprints not too far from the

entrance. Whatever caused them, sent the Pteranodons this way. Causing a disturbance."

"What kind of footprints?" Sahara wondered. "Tyrannosaurus? Velociraptor?"

"No. It's not from these lands. It's something from afar."

"More invaders?" Tor-Zar questioned. "Can't be. We ran off the others."

"These footprints do not belong to those like us." The Tribes Leader said. "Humans. They seem feral. Paw-like. But more liken to ours. Visceral to be described."

Tor-Zar nodded. He extended his arm toward the Leader and they shook.

"I'll do what I can to track this thing down. Keep the lands protected."

"We know you will."

II

THE FIND

Tor-Zar and Kujo both went deeper into the wilderness, tracking the footprints. Sahara stayed with the Tribe just in case the suspected anomaly returned toward the tribes' land. Kujo sniffed the grounds, moving further into the forest. Tor-Zar knelt, rubbing the footprint.

"What is this?" He questioned.

His attention was snatched quickly b Kujo's roaring. Tor-Zar ran toward the roars, finding Kujo staring down three velociraptors. The raptors' hide peaked green and blue in the sunlight. They snarled at Tor-Zar and Kujo. Tor-Zar held his spear tightly, snarling back at the raptors. The raptors screeched and attacked Tor-Zar and Kujo. The battle was not a fierce one, due to the skills of Tor-Zar and his spear. Kujo's own strength was enough to trample over one of the raptor's bodies, while lunging on the other, snapping its neck. Tor-Zar ran toward the incoming raptor, with its claws out and mouth open. Tor-Zar swiped the spear against the raptor, knocking it on the ground near one of the large trees.

"Stay down." Tor-Zar said.

The raptor rose and snarled. Yet, the raptor was caught up in the mouth of a larger predator. Tor-Zar and Kujo raised their heads above, seeing a tyrannosaurus rex staring them down while chewing and swallowing the raptor whole. The two stepped back as the T-Rex set its eyes upon them. Kujo growled, Tor-Zar held his spear tightly.

The T-Rex roared and rushed the two, knocking them on opposite sides of its body. Kujo raised up, lunging atop the T-Rex, clawing and biting its back. Tor-Zar arose, ramming the spear into the T-Rex's leg. The leg went up and came down, shoving Tor-Zar onto the ground once more. The T-Rex shook itself, causing Kujo to lose his grip and slip off. The T-Rex turned toward Kujo, with its mouth open and the teeth covered with saliva and blood. The T-Rex leaned down toward Kujo and quickly, Tor-Zar lunged the spear, impacting the T-Rex in its head. The dinosaur roared in pain, shaking its head as the spear fell to the ground. Kujo stood up and clawed the leg while Tor-Zar snatched the spear and swiped it across the T-Rex's chest. The large dinosaur walked off into the forest with only the echoing sounds of its roars and footsteps heard.

Tor-Zar patted him and Kujo went over toward him, looking for wounds. Tor-Zar smirked, patting Kujo.

"Did good."

From behind them arrived the Tribe with Sahara. Tor-Zar stood up as she approached him, seeing some minor cuts on his arms and chest. Kujo had some minor wounds of his own. Sahara looked around, seeing several of the nearby trees were knocked down.

"What happened?"

"Came across some raptors. Dealt with them before a T-Rex showed up. Me and Kujo dealt with it and it went off into the forest."

"What of the creature?" The Tribes Leader asked. "Did you manage to find what caused the footprints?"

"Not yet."

As the leader and Tor-Zar spoke, Sahara caught a glimpse of something moving around the trees nearby. She took several steps forward to see and as she did, a creature lunged out toward her. She ducked as the creature flew over her, sliding on the ground. The others witness it and band together, seeing the creature for what it is. It stood over seven feet, with grey and black hairs covering its body. The snout spewing with saliva and its yellow eyes frightened the tribes' people.

"What is that?" The leader asked.

"I've heard of their kind before." Tor-Zar said. "It's a lycan."

"How did it get here?" Sahara wondered. "There aren't any wolves on this land."

"It found a way. Most likely the same pathway as the invaders."

The leader grabbed his spear and ran toward the werewolf for an impale attack. The lycan dodged he attacked, snatching the spear and breaking it in half before swiping the leader back toward his people. The werewolf roared, expressing its physique and strength. Tor-Zar, Sahara, and Kujo stood in front of the tribes' people facing the creature.

"We'll have to take it down." Sahara said.

"I agree." Tor-Zar replied.

"You dare attempt to strike me!" The lycan spoke.

"You can talk?" Tor-Zar said. "Makes things better. State your name, creature."

"My name is of no concern. I have finally found the land spoken of across the ages. Now, I will rid this place of you and your kind. I will rule amongst the creature of this land and in time, my kind will rise again."

"Not before we stop you." Sahara said, raising her spear.

III

AN OPEN WORLD

Tor-Zar collided with the lycan, whose claws were able to withstand Tor-Zar's spear. Sahara and Kujo jumped into the battle as the tribes' people watched on. Tor-Zar was knock across the ground, leaving Kujo and Sahara to face the lycan. The lycan's strength was more than impressive, as he easily defeated Kujo with several swips to the back and lunged atop Sahara, smashing his weight against her own, shoving her into the dirt. The lycan roared at the tribes' people before Tor-Zar stood up, holding his staff.

"That weapon will have no effect on me." The lycan said.

Tor-Zar paused and nodded, dropping the spear into the ground and pulling out two daggers from his boots. He held them up, facing the creature.

"Your move."

The lycan clashed its claws against the two blades. Pulling his hand back, seeing his own blood. The lycan was confused as he looked back and forth between his hand and the blades.

"What are those made of?"

"Solidium. Why do you ask?"

"Not possible. I cannot be wounded. I am Lycano."

"Your name is Lycano?" Tor-Zar noted. "Well, you have a choice, Lycano. Either leave this land in peace or die here and be food for the vultures."

"I cannot die. I am beyond this land."

Lycano took off into the woods, only letting out a small howl before vanishing into the forest. Tor-Zar placed his blades back into their sheaths and went to check on Sahara and Kujo. Both of which were well, with only slight wounds. They returned with the tribe back to their lands. There, Tor-Zar went and mediated, with the two blades laying on the ground besides him with the blood of Lycano still intact. Sahara entered the cave where Tor-Zar sat and kneeled front of him as his eyes opened. She looked at the blades and saw the blood, shaking her head.

"You let him go."

"He had a choice and he made it."

"What if he comes back? What if he's not alone next time?"

"We can take him. Besides, I know for a fact that's not the last we've seen of him."

CROSSBREED: A DARK TITAN UNIVERSE EVENT

I

MEETING OF THE MINDS

General Rilla and his Fellowship stand inside their lair. Some of the nubreeds are healing after the events with the Steelers. While they stood, waiting for their visitor, Cosmic Card approached Rilla, looking around at the others.

"Who is coming to meet us?"

"A stranger from another place. He seeks to aid us in moving those traitors out of our way. Giving opportunity to our cause."

"He a nubreed like us?"

"He's something else. Neither human nor nubreed. Otherworldly is the word I would use to describe him."

The doors of the lair opened, catching everyone's attention. The visitor walked in, dressed in nearly all black with some dark-blue colors on his apparel. He wore a black duster with blue linings. passing through an aisle of nubreeds with their eyes on him. He casually walked forward as the doors closed behind him. His eyes were set on what's in front of him and that was Rilla himself. The Stranger stood in front of Rilla as his Fellowship circled him. The Stranger nodded.

"You've come." Rilla said. "I respect that."

"It is of an important cause and I am happy to help."

"Before we discuss terms, you didn't tell me your name."

"I am known in my world and amongst my people as Romanus Dakingor."

"Dakingor?" Rilla said. "Sounds strong."

"That is what I believe it to be. But, there are others who see it as an opposing force for their well-being."

"You seek something else in this agreement of ours?"

"I have a proposal for you and your Fellowship."

"Do tell."

"I'll help you eliminate the Yonderers and you can aid me in taking out my adversaries."

"Are you adversaries the same as you or are they of another kind?"

"They are of my kind. Yet, they are betrayers to our cause. Desiring to live like the others outside our ranks."

"Sounds like the Yonderers. Hmm, we are in the same boat. Let's talk."

II

STRIKE FIRST

The Yonderers sat inside the Yonderer Mansion with Professor Edge instructing them on the aftereffects of the Steelers. The whole team was present to hear Edge's words. Through the teaching, a rumbling sound echoed overhead. Startling the team as they prepared themselves and went outside, Edge stood still, mediating as he looked up.

"Someone's here."

"Who's here?" Lois Frost asked. "More Steelers?"

"No. Something otherworldly."

The team ran outside, only to find themselves staring at a small, yet powerful force. Professor Edge went out with them, seeing the group standing in front of them. Edge could sense their power. It was strong. Stronger than most of the nubreeds he's come across.

"Who are they?" Lois asked. "Are they nubreeds?"

"No, they're not nubreeds. There's something else."

The group stood a dozen strong. Walking through them to the front was Romanus. There, he looked out toward the Yonderers and scoffed.

"This is who Rilla is up against." Romanus whispered. "Shame."

"Who are you?" Edge asked.

"We are a people from another place. Far from here."
Romanus said. "We've come to discuss terms with the kind called
'nubreeds'."

"Terms? What kind of terms?"

"My kind see yours as a primary enemy. Therefore, in our
culture, it is nature for one to annihilate the other. Only one
bloodline shall remain. The other must be eviscerated
permanently."

"We do not that those words kindly." Edge said. "If you wish
to threaten us, perhaps you should've gone with your attacks
already.'

"Fair point."

Romanus waved his hands, signaling the attack as his army ran
toward the Yonderers for the fight. The young team was prepared
as Edge led them into the battle. Lois and Valinor collided with
the front liners, quickly taking them down. However, there were
three larger ones standing before the Yonderers. Surf went for an
attack and it didn't even stumble them. Emerald went with an
attack of his own, trying to tire out the unkinds. Romanus savored
the battle before his eyes, seeing Crystalax making a move toward
him, Romanus held his hand up freezing the Yonderer in his place
and walked away before he fell to the ground face-first.

"Weakness is a disgust." Romanus said.

He looked out toward the battle, seeing his army being quickly
defeated. Romanus hated the idea of losing a battle, much less a
war. Romanus shook his head, thinking of the timing and the
current idea.

"This is not going to last long. Never was meant to. A
distraction is all that we needed."

Instead, he took matters into his own hands by creating a
slight power surge and attacking the Yonderer Base, blowing a
large hole through the front. The blast knocked the Yonderers and
Edge to the ground. With the explosion, Romanus took his leave

with the followers who remained. Once the debris cleared out, Edge scouted the area, seeing Romanus had vanished and the others who were with him had also gone.

"Professor, what shall we do?" Valinor questioned. "Won't they be back?"

"We need to do some studying. See where they truly come from. Why they're here and what they want."

"And what are we going to do once we have the answers?" Lois asked. "Track them down and do the same to them?"

"We are not like that, Frost. You know our operations well. Best not to let your emotions tamper with your decisions."

"I have to agree with the lady on this one." Valinor said. "What are we going to do once we find out who they truly are?"

"We will get to that once everything is in place." Edge answered. "Right now, we repair and prepare."

Elsewhere, Halo Lock and his liege of Unkinds move through the countryside of Illinois. From there, Cygnus, one of Halo Lock's trusted soldiers looked up at a sign. He pointed with clarity.

"My lord, is that the name of the place?"

Halo Lock looked toward the sign, seeing the word "Chicago". He nodded.

"That is the place written. The place where the Yonderers dwell."

"Then we're not far." Aquila, Halo Lock's wife spoke. "We'll finally get our answers."

"We shall indeed receive answers. "Halo Lock replied. "I hope they are the answers we have sought after."

III

THE PLAN IS SIMPLE

Romanus returned to the Fellowship Lair, seeing Rilla speaking with his nubreed followers. He moved with a fast pace in his steps, as the eyes of the fellowship turned toward him. Inching closer, Rilla spotted him and stepped forward.

"What has happened?" Rilla asked.

"I paid a trip to these Yonderers. I've caused a slight disturbance for them which should benefit our cause."

"I see. Are they dead?"

"No. only did some damage to their home. The message is clear. Once Halo Lock and his Liege arrive to the Yonderers, they will be the enemy and the war will begin."

Rilla smirked.

"Giving way for the two of us to enter at a moment's notice. Let them destroy each other. Then, we'll enter and eliminate the surviving force."

"Good to know." Romanus said, rubbing his chin.

"I must ask, why go through all of this? Seeking to prove yourself to your kind?"

"I'm the rightful ruler of my people. Halo Lock isn't capable of leading our people into a better future."

"Halo Lock, I must ask. What is his power? How does he lead your people in such a strong devotion?"

"He has his ways. Him and his wife are their king and queen to an extent."

"You seek to be king."

"More so their emperor. I know how to lead my people and rule them well. We can do things that will make us even better than we were on our ancient home world."

"And what of your home world this day?"

"Barren. Unlivable. We sought a better path and better world. We found this one. Later, we discovered there were others already here. A melting pot of such kinds. Halo and I disagreed on our plans for coming here. Most of our people sided with him. A few others placed their loyalty to me."

"And this Halo Lock picked his Liege alongside his wife and began their travels across the earth. As did you."

"Yes. We went separate paths. Although, they will always fear our reunion."

"I'll be there to witness such an event. If a battle does become of it, you have me, and the Fellowship on your side."

"Just as I will stand with you against those Yonderers."

"Will you stand with us after you've ended Halo Lock and his Liege?' Rilla questioned.

"Well yes."

"Excellent spirit you have. We'll find out once we're on the battlefield. But for now, we wait."

IV

YONDERERS OR UNKINDS?

Edge and the Yonderers all sat in the main room of the base, reflecting on their encounter with the Unkinds. A day had passed, with several of the young nubreeds repairing the wall of the base with their abilities of speed and strength. The next day after Edge had compiled every known information regarding the interstellar species he could find. Including reading an article about a farmer who encountered their landing and even spoke with them. Stating they were interested in nubreeds.

"We must be ready for their return." Edge said.

"Return?" Emerald questioned. "What would give them a reason to bother us again?"

A sound of commotion came from the outside, leading them all back into the front where they set their eyes upon Halo Lock and his Liege. The Yonderers stood guard with Edge in front. He saw their appearance and stature. He knew they were unkinds.

"Are they?" Lois asked.

"They are."

"We've been looking for you." Halo Lock said, stepping forward toward the steps. "I am Halo Lock and this is my liege. We've been seeking the ones called nubreeds. We've traveled a great length."

"We know who you are!" Valinor yelled. "Your kind attacked

us."

"Our kind?" Aquila said. "Are you sure they were one of us?"

"There were enough." Edge said. "The one who led them talked of domination. Our extinction."

"You speak of Romanus. He is one of us in species. But not in allegiance."

"Yet, your all unkinds. You all seek the same goal."

"We do not."

"Payback must be given." Emerald said.

"Is this what you want?" Halo asked. "We only came to learn of your kind. Not to fight."

"This Romanus has another motive than you and your followers." Edge said.

"Again. He is one of us. Yet, not with us."

Edge walked down the stairs, facing Halo. He looked into his eyes, seeing similarity of the stars above. The Yonderers stood, waiting for the signal as were Halo's liege. They stood still. Each side waiting for a move. Edge nodded as did Halo.

"Let us talk."

"Thank you." Halo said.

Edge escorted Halo and his liege into the Yonderer home with the team keeping their eyes locked on them, entering the home behind them. Edge led them to the main room where he and Halo spoke concerning their differences and what had transpired with Romanus' earlier visit. Outside of the room, Aquila sat with Lois.

"Are you the queen of this place?" Aquila asked.

"Not exactly."

"There must be some form of royalty here. I assume the man talking with my husband is the king."

"No. Edge is not a king. He's a professor."

"He teaches you? All of you?"

"Yes."

"What about?"

"How to live in a world where others refuse to accept you for who you are."

"Hmm. Sounds like us."

"I guess everyone deals with it in some way."

"It's nature to many kinds across the planes."

Edge and Halo sit conformably at the table, discussing their views on the nubreeds and unkinds. Halo told Edge of their history. How they left their previous home world and came to this world. Seeking a place to refuge and later call home. Edge questioned Halo on their enthusiasm to meet nubreeds. Halo replied by stating the nubreed are not that different in nature to the unkinds. Although, there is more of a royalty mindset and culture to the unkinds as opposed to the general civilized nature of some nubreeds.

"What do you plan to do about Romanus?" Edge questioned. "I know he's not working alone."

"He has his followers. They do whatever he commands."

"I wasn't speaking of his followers."

"I'm not understanding. You mean he's working with someone else. Someone of his nature?"

"I know a guy. He's very similar to Romanus in every way. Aside from the ambush."

"Is he a nubreed?"

"He is. General Rilla is his name. a militant nubreed. Desires for all on the earth to submit to the nubreed species. With him as their leader."

"You believe Romanus and Rilla are working together. Trying to get us to fight each other while they sneak in and attack at the last moment."

"It's a plan Rilla would use to his advantage."

"Then we must prepare ourselves for the coming fight." Halo declared. "I will tell my liege everything. Get them prepared."

"I will do the same with my students. It's good we see things the same."

Edge and Halo walked out to their respective sides, telling them of their discussion and next phase of plans against Romanus and Rilla. Halo and his liege left, seeking to find Romanus and his followers. Meanwhile, Edge gathered the Yonderers together, preparing them for the fight against Rilla and Romanus. Lois looked around the room before turning to Edge.

"I think we might need some extra assist."

"I have an idea." Edge said. "Would you accompany me?"

"Sure. Where are we going?"

"To ask someone for help."

V

TERROR AND HORROR

Edge and Frost traveled further out of Chicago, reaching the base of John Terror. Exiting the car as they walked toward the door, Lois was a slight hesitant. She wondered if Terror would help them in this battle. Edge declared Terror would because he himself is a nubreed and will be on Romanus' radar eventually if he is not stopped. Edge knocked on the door and it opened.

"What are you doing here?" Terror asked, standing at the door.

"John, we need your help." Edge said. "It is of a great matter."

"Greater than the Steelers?"

"Much greater."

Terror nodded.

"Let's talk. Only because you're a decent man."

They entered the lair, seeing Carl Prater and Jade Horror working. Edge nodded with a smirk.

"I see you have company."

"They can hear whatever you're proposing."

"Proposing?" Jade said. "What's going on?"

"They're a new species upon this world. They call themselves the Unkinds."

"And?" Terror said.

"They want all nubreeds extinct."

"For what purpose would they come for us? Why not the humans first?"

"Because we'll panic faster." Carl noted. "It's only the truth."

"They have a leader. In fact, two leaders."

"I see. And you want myself to align with you and your team once again to face these leaders?"

"No. only one. The other leader will be assisting us with a team of his own. Not all of the Unkinds share the same motives."

"Ah." Terror scoffed. "Good to hear."

"That is not all. General Rilla and his Fellowship are aiding them in the fight against us."

"Rilla again, huh." Terror said. "Can't the guy give it a rest."

"Unfortunately, no." Lois added. "He believes that helping the Unkinds eliminate us will give him the opportunity of achieving what he craves."

"It's a tactic he would use."

"So, will you help us against Rilla and the Unkinds?"

Terror stood by his desk, he looked over to Carl and Jade. Carl nodded, Jade gave him a shrug. Terror hung his head and grinned.

"Hell, as long as this doesn't interfere with my work, I'll help once again."

"We appreciate it highly."

"He's not going alone." Jade said. "I'm coming too."

"More nubreeds the better." Edge noted. "Is he coming along as well?"

"Me? No. I'll stay here. Keep the place secure. Don't worry, John."

"I won't. You know what to do." Terror said. "Jade, let's get out gear."

Terror and Horror gathered their gear, dressed in their combat attire. Jade's new attire was sleek and slimier to Terror's own, except the insignia on her torso was a mix between the letters J and H. Lois spotted it out, pointing.

"I see you have one of your own."

"I wasn't sharing his."

"We're ready."

"We'll head back to the others. Prep for what's ahead and find out where Rilla and Romanus are located."

"You sure they won't draw us out? I mean that's what Rilla intends to do."

"You're positive on that?" Lois wondered. "Rilla isn't that ignorant of the methods."

"What better way to bring out the Yonderers and this other Unkind leader without a call to challenge."

"Right now, we discuss matters with the team. Deal with Rilla's possible challenge later."

VI

TWO SIDES, ONE FUTURE

Edge and Lois returned to the Yonderer homestead with Terror and Jade riding behind them on their motorcycles. They entered the base, seeing the Yonderers themselves. Terror, once more, found himself aligning with others like himself and he smirked.

"At this again aren't we." Terror said.

"Everyone, listen." Edge said. "We will take the battle to those unkinds. Halo Lock has already agreed to help us. As we will be helping him and his followers."

"How are we going to do all of this?" Valinor asked. "I mean, are we going to just call out those guys or something?"

A loud burst erupted from the outside. Terror sighed as the Yonderers ran to see it. Terror walked out of the doors behind them, seeing Rilla, the Fellowship, and the Unkinds led by Romanus standing in front of him and the Yonderers. The gate to the homestead was destroyed by their entry.

"Those the guys?" Terror asked.

"Yes." Edge replied. "That is them."

"They don't look tough."

"Cullen." Rilla yelled. "It appears we have found ourselves in another conflict. One so of bloodlines."

"Why align with them, Raymus? Why not go against them

and their plan?"

"Romanus shares my motives. In order to achieve victory, we must first eliminate the opposing obstacles in the course. Such as your Yonderers are in my way, the weak king of the Unkinds is in the path of Romanus."

Romanus looked around, not seeing Halo Lock or his liege anywhere on the Yonderer grounds. The sight of it enraged him. Yet, he kept calm."

"Where could he be?" Romanus questioned.

"You've made the decision to attack us at our home?"

"It's a better fit for it. I mean, the city's already seen enough damage from our conflict with the Steelers and McKnight. Chicago doesn't need to suffer once again for you to get my point."

"We don't have to do this." Edge stated. "There's no need for us to fight one another. Not again."

"You don't always get what you desire, old friend."

From the sky cracked down a large bolt of lightning. Within the lightning was Halo Lock and his liege. Romanus stumbled in his steps as Rilla and his Fellowship looked on. Halo's eyes were set on Romanus as he and the liege stood at the side of the Yonderers. Terror stared at them.

"These are the good ones?"

"The ones we know of." Lois said.

"Let's see what they can do."

Romanus stepped forward as his mouth foamed toward Halo Lock.

"This is my time, Halotarus!"

"It didn't have to be this way." Halo said. "However, you've made your choice and we've made ours."

Romanus screamed in rage as his followers rushed toward Halo Lock and his liege. Rilla noticed the beginning and signaled the Fellowship to attack the Yonderers. Edge did the same as the

Yonderers rushed into battle with Terror and Horror joining them. Rilla and Romanus stood back and watched the ongoing fight. Edge did the same, keeping his eyes on the two leaders. Valinor and Frost took the fight to Cosmic Card and Mistress Destroyer. Omega Thunder and X-Manta were clashing with Emerald and Crystalax in the battle of the elements. Thunder and mineral colliding. The Marine fought off against The Surf. The rushing of the sudden waters were only a brush of air toward the Marine. Eerie used her supernatural powers against the sheer force of Gale's wind. Jackhammer did what he could to catch up to Magic Carpet's speed in the air. Halo's liege fought fiercely against the Followers of Romanus. Brutality against those of their own kind. Terror and Horror were in between the battle. Fighting against both nubreeds and unkinds alike.

"This is slightly different than the Steelers." Jade said.

"Doesn't matter." Terror said. "They're still the enemy."

"Is this what you wanted?" Rilla asked Romanus. "To see your own kind decimate one another?"

"If it achieves victory, it must be done."

Rilla nodded with a grin.

"You are fit to rule your people. Just as I am fit to rule over the nubreeds."

"However, Rilla, I cannot allow the nubreeds to continue to exist once I become king of the Unkinds."

"Where has this talk come from?"

"It was always my plan. To rule over my own and to dominate the rest. The nubreeds are the perennial threat. Such as you to me."

Romanus blasted Rilla against the ruins of the gate, shocking Edge. Romanus did the same toward the battle and Edge. Rilla arose, his eyes surging with energy as he levitated into the air above the battle.

"You have destroyed your chances!"

Romanus watched Rilla in the air and quickly Romanus was taken down by Halo Lock, who stood over him with his foot on his neck.

"Is this how your rule shall be?" Romanus jolted. "Your foot on our people's throat?"

"That is your definition of rule. Not mine."

"Stand aside, Unkind King!" Rilla yelled from above.

"Leave Romanus to me. We will deliver him a just judgment."

"I cannot abide with an attack on myself nor my kind by any other race. This ends now."

"Rilla, cease yourself!" Edge yelled. "Do not harm him!"

"You ally with him, Cullen?!"

"I align with the good I see. Halo Lock is good. Let him deal with Romanus in their own way."

"What makes you sure this will ot happen again?"

"Because I am their king." Halo declared. "In my rule, such actions will not take place nor require such a sheer force of retaliation. This is my statement toward you. You and the nubreeds will never have to concern yourself with the threats of any unkind. If they do bring a threat, they are not of my service and I will not come to aid them. They will be destroyed by their adversaries."

Rilla sighed and came back to the ground, standing over Romanus and facing Edge and Halo Lock.

"I will see to your words, Unkind King."

"They are trustworthy."

"This battle between us, our ideologies is not over, Cullen."

"There's no need for violence. Not today."

"As you say. For if I knew I was being set up for betrayal, I would've killed Romanus sooner than we had come."

Rilla looked out to the battle, rallying his Fellowship as they took their leave. Some defeated. Few victorious. Halo's liege gathered Romanus' followers and took them afar off.

"That's it?" Terror joked. "It's over already?!"

Afterwards, Edge spoke with Halo in detail, concerning their matters and ways between nubreeds and unkinds.

"If something like this happens again, we will come and assist you." Halo said.

"I appreciate such an offer, but, I believe the Yonderers can handle threats like these themselves."

"I wasn't referring to Rilla and his followers. I mean the others out there. Those 'risen heroes' the humans speak of. What happens if they choose to come across your path?"

"I'm not sure that will happen."

"As you are aware, never take something such as a possible war as just a theory."

Edge nodded.

"Duly noted. Where are you and your liege off to?"

"To a place where we can live peacefully and where I can rule in servitude."

"I wish you the best."

"And I you, Professor of the nubreeds."

Halo and his liege left the Yonderer homestead. Edge remained in his office. Calm as the Yonderers went back to their studies and training. Terror and Horror returned to the base. Elsewhere, General Rilla spoke to his Fellowship about the current possibilities of a larger war involving nubreeds, unkinds, and humanity. Rilla began preparing them for the cause without haste. He knew it was only a matter of when, not if it would come to pass.

ABOUT THE AUTHOR

Ty'Ron W. C. Robinson II is the author of several works of fiction. Including the *Dark Titan Universe Saga* series, *The Haunted City Saga, EverWar Universe, Symbolum Venatores, Frightened!,* and more. More information pertaining to the author and stories can be found at darktitanentertainment.com.

Twitter:@TyronRobinsonII

Twitter: @DarkTitan_
Instagram: @darktitanentertainment